Killer Wedding Cake

A Daphne Martin Cake Mystery

Gayle Trent

Grace Abraham Publishing

Bristol, Virginia

Gayle Trent
Grace Abraham Publishing
Bristol, Virginia 24202
www.gayletrent.com

Publisher's Note: This is a work of fiction. Names, characters, places, and incidents are a product of the author's imagination. Locales and public names are sometimes used for atmospheric purposes. Any resemblance to actual people, living or dead, or to businesses, companies, events, institutions, or locales is completely coincidental.

Book Layout © 2014 BookDesignTemplates.com

Killer Wedding Cake/Gayle Trent. -- 1st ed.
ISBN 0-9741090-9-6

Cover art by Wicked Smart Designs
http://www.wickedsmartdesigns.com/

Editing by Jeni Chappelle
http://www.jenichappelle.com/

PRAISE FOR THE DAPHNE MARTIN CAKE MYSTERIES

"One day I found myself happily reading . . . mysteries by Gayle Trent. If she can win me over . . . she's got a great future." —Dean Koontz, #1 New York Times bestselling author

"Both Gayle and I are fascinated with the ins and outs of baking and decorating and the convoluted backstories that make it all so exciting; the crème de la crème for a mystery writer. A must read for cake bakers and anyone who has ever spent creative time in the kitchen!" – Kerry Vincent, Hall of Fame Sugar Artist, Oklahoma State Sugar Art Show Director, Television Personality

"Entertaining…and tasty read" – Entertainment Weekly

"For people who love a tasty cake and a cozy murder mystery, Murder Takes the Cake is a delicious read." - Suzanne Pitner, Suite101.com

"The breezy story line is fun to follow…Daphne is a solid lead character as she follows the murder recipe one step at a time to the delight of sub-genre readers." – Harriet Klausner, The Mystery Gazette

4 · GAYLE TRENT

"I absolutely was startled to find out whodunnit at the end and it was not one of those lame-o choices so the author could hurry and finish up. I could identify with Daphne's relationship with her family. I think this was the part I liked best. Daphne has a cautious and teeth gritting relationship with her mother, a loving warm one with her father and her sister. And the cake baking and decorating!!! I didn't get the recipes in the copy I reviewed, so will get the book just for those. This is one of my criteria for a cozy, it makes me want to learn how to do the activity that's the basis of the character and story......This one makes me want to learn how to decorate cakes. Four frosted beans!" – Vixen's Daily Reads

"...a sweetly satisfying mystery that'll have you licking your lips for more!" – Christine Verstraete, Searching for a Starry Night, a Miniature Art Mystery

"Murder Takes the Cake has all the right ingredients for a delicious read." – Ellen Crosby, author of The Bordeaux Betrayal

OTHER BOOKS IN THE DAPHNE MARTIN CAKE MYSTERIES

MURDER TAKES THE CAKE
DEAD PAN
KILLER SWEET TOOTH
BATTERED TO DEATH

KILLER WEDDING CAKE

CHAPTER ONE

For what seemed like the millionth time, I sat at my computer, scrolling through images of wedding cakes. I decorate cakes for a living, but this was my wedding cake.

And Ben's, of course. Our wedding cake.

So I'd been agonizing over the design for months. Now the wedding was less than two weeks away, and I absolutely had to get the design nailed down and start making the decorations.

I heard a knock at my side door. It had to be a friend or family member. A stranger would've rung the front doorbell. I pushed away from the desk and went through the kitchen to answer the door. My sister Violet, neighbor Myra, and friend China were standing in my carport. I was concerned. Had you known these three, you'd have been worried too.

Myra pushed ahead of the other two and came into the kitchen. She was an attractive widow in her early- to mid-sixties who lived in the house directly to my left.

"This is one of them interventions, Daphne. We're worried that you're never going to get your wedding cake picked out and we'll all be standing around eating snack cakes or doughnuts at the reception, and you'll be crying because you didn't get your cake made."

China, an older lady who's always reminded me of a cross between Willie Nelson and a wood nymph, gave Myra a sharp look. "We don't give a fig about what we'll be eating at the reception." She patted my arm. "It's you we're concerned about."

Violet merely smiled. I didn't know whether the other two had induced her to tag along on this "intervention" or if it was the other way around. Either way, my sister knew her arguments would be made by the two veterans. She didn't have to say a word.

"So, let's get to it," Myra said. "Let's design your wedding cake."

"Actually, I was just looking at cakes online." I invited the trio to join me in my home office-slash-guest room.

I sat back down at the computer and scrolled through the images. I was uncomfortable having the three interveners literally breathing down the back of my neck, but I knew they meant well.

"Go back! Go back!" Myra leaned over my shoulder and pointed at the screen. "I liked that one with the purple flowers on it. Let's get a better look at that."

"But her colors are pink and white," said Violet.

"She could do purple and pink."

"I think that purple one is a little too showy." China raised both her eyebrows and her shoulders.

Myra huffed. "You think everything's too showy."

Granted, Myra and China were as different as night and day with regard to showiness. Myra liked to wear trendier clothing while China was happy with her jeans and flannel shirts. Myra got her hair done on a regular basis, which included covering her gray and adding highlights, at Tanya's Tremendous Tress Taming Salon. China's iron gray braids hung to her waist, and I'd only seen her hair styled differently once—when a group of us had gone to see some Elvis impersonators.

China pointed out a white-on-white design. "That's simple and elegant. I like it."

"How about that one that looks like a wedding dress?" Myra asked.

"All it would take is for one of the men to drink too much and go to wanting to eat the boobies."

Myra gasped. "China York! I cannot believe you just said boobies!"

I couldn't believe it myself, but it was awfully funny. And China was right. I didn't think a wedding dress cake was the way to go.

"That's it," Violet said softly. "The five-tier blush colored cake with the white and rose colored accents."

"You're right." I enlarged the image. "That's beautiful. And I can embellish it with the Australian string work I've been practicing since that class I took in the spring."

I spun around in my chair and looked at Vi. The younger of the two of us, she was blonde, dainty, and bubbly. I was none of the above. It was like I was her polar opposite—tall, athletic build, brown hair and eyes, and rather serious.

"That's it." She gave me a nod. "That's your cake."

"I know."

She laughed and hugged me. Then I hugged Myra and China too.

"Why didn't you guys do this a month ago?" I asked.

"Well, we thought for sure you had this under control," Myra said. "But when Violet told me at the Save-A-Buck this morning that you didn't have a clue as to how you wanted to do your cake, we thought it was time to step in."

So it had been Violet's idea—or at least her suggestion. I squinted at her, and she gave me the charming little pixie expression that had, thus far, kept her from ever getting a speeding ticket. I merely shook my head. I was, in fact, happy to have the burden lifted and to have chosen a design for the wedding cake.

Steve Franklin, the manager of the Save-A-Buck, must've had a sixth sense that someone was talking about his store because he called only seconds after Myra mentioned it.

"Hi, Steve," I said. "What can I do for you?"

"We're getting low on baked goods."

The Save-A-Buck didn't have a bakery, so I took cakes, cookies, brownies, candies, doughnuts, and sometimes breads to the store to be sold on consignment. If and when the items were sold—and they almost always were—I got a check.

"I'd like eight round, single-layer cakes—six birthday and two plain," he continued.

"Four white, four chocolate?"

"Yeah, that'll work. I'd also like a few boxes of chocolate chip cookies, some oatmeal raisin cookies, and some snickerdoodles."

"How about brownies?"

"Sure. They always sell well."

"When do you need these?" I asked.

"Let's see…it's Tuesday, so can you have everything here by Thursday?"

If I baked around the clock, I could. "Yeah. I probably won't be at the store first thing Thursday morning, but I'll be there as soon as possible."

"Thanks, Daphne. I appreciate you."

"Sounds like a big order," Myra said when I ended the call.

I nodded. "Apparently, the Save-A-Buck is completely out of baked goods."

"We'd better go and let you get to it." China nodded toward the door. "After you, ladies."

Myra acted as if she wasn't entirely ready to leave, but she did. Violet kissed me on the cheek and said she'd give me a call later. And China told me to let her know if I needed anything.

After seeing them to the door, I washed my hands at the sink, got out my favorite blue mixing bowl, and decided to start with the brownies. If I baked two large pans, I could cut them into two-inch by two-inch squares, and have enough to make five half-dozen boxes. I set the oven to preheat and then got out my pan, a large spoon, my brownie recipe, and the ingredients I needed.

As I mixed up the brownies, I thought about how far I'd come these past few months in Brea Ridge. I'd been working as a secretary for a government housing regulatory agency in northeast Tennessee when my ex-husband Todd had fired a pistol at me.

What grievous crime had I committed to deserve being shot at, you ask? I'd gone four-tenths of a mile out of my way to a bookstore on my commute home from work. I hadn't asked to visit the bookstore—hadn't got Todd's approval—and when he'd checked the odometer on my car, he knew I'd gone somewhere other than to work and back.

I'd known by the time I got home that I'd be in trouble. Todd had always checked my odometer when I arrived home from work. But at some point during that day, I'd decided I was tired of it. I wanted to go to the bookstore, and I did. You want to know what book I bought?

Regaining Your Self-Respect: A Ten-Step Plan.

So I'd stood up to Todd and declared, "Yes! I went to the bookstore!"

And he'd pulled out a pistol and shot at some point slightly above and to the left of my head. I admit I hadn't seen that coming. I'd been expecting him to slap me or shove me, not pull out a gun. I'd called the police, and Todd had been arrested and eventually sentenced to seven years in prison.

Even then, I'd stayed in Tennessee for another five years. By the end of that time, I'd worked twenty years at the housing agency and could retire with enough retirement benefits to return to Virginia, buy a small house, and operate Daphne's Delectable Cakes out of my home. Even better, I got to spend more time with my adorable twin nephew and niece, Lucas and Leslie.

And I'd reconnected with Ben Jacobs, my high school sweetheart. Ben had never married, and I knew he was the man I should've married twenty years ago. Dating Todd and ultimately marrying him had been the worst mistake of my life.

But I wasn't dwelling on past mistakes today. I was making brownies. And I'd finally chosen a design for our wedding cake and could concentrate on that as I worked.

From the corner of my eye, I noticed Sparrow—the one-eyed Persian cat I'd inherited with the house—run by in a streak of gray and white fur. She was a tad on the feral side, and I imagine it had freaked her out to have so many people here earlier this morning. She must be on a recon mission to make sure our guests were gone.

"It's just you and me again, kid!"

Soon it would be her, me, Ben, and Ben's golden retriever, Sally. He and I had introduced the pair a few weeks ago. That had ended with Sparrow hissing from beneath my bed and Sally peeking under the dust ruffle wagging her entire lower half while she barked excitedly. Ben and I had decided to try again later. Maybe after the honeymoon.

I spread the brownie batter into the pan, opened the oven door, and slid the pan inside. The oven was cold. It wasn't that it hadn't heated up all the way yet—it was completely cold. And here I was with a pan of brownie batter that I needed to get baked. I called Myra.

"Don't tell me you've changed your mind about the cake already," she said, by way of answering.

"No. My oven won't heat. I have a pan of brownie batter and no oven."

"Well, bring the pan over here. I'll go ahead and preheat my oven. What do you need it set on—three-fifty?"

"Yes, please. Thank you!" I ended the call, put a lid on my brownie pan, and hurried out the door to Myra's house.

Bruno met me at the door. He was a tan Chihuahua who could've slept in one of my shoes. Myra had met the teensy terror a few months ago when he'd barked and growled at her from her front porch. She'd called me frantic because "this vicious dog" wouldn't let her into her house. I'd taken over a piece of ham, and it had calmed the savage beastie right down. She began feeding him, and he stayed. He still acted as if he owned the place, but he had a more legitimate claim to do so now.

"Hello, Bruno," I said.

He danced around on his back legs, thinking I had a treat for him because I usually did. This time, however, I'd only thought to bring my pan of brownies.

"Sorry, buddy. I'll get you something when I go back."

"Put the pan there on the counter and come take a load off while we wait for the oven to finish pre-heating," Myra said.

I did as she said, but I touched the front of the oven as I passed by to make sure it was getting hot. Sorry, but I was feeling paranoid. Thank goodness, the oven was warm.

Then I went in and collapsed onto the sofa beside Myra.

"Honey, you look plumb tuckered out," she said.

"It's not that I'm tired. I'm just aggravated. I don't know what's wrong with my oven."

"It's probably the heating element. It'll be all right."

"Are you sure you don't mind me using your oven? I'll pay you in a box of brownies." You wouldn't know it from her trim frame, but Myra loved sweets.

"I didn't mind to begin with, but I doubly don't mind now."

Bruno raced into the living room and hopped onto the sofa between us.

"I need to make two pans—one to go in as soon as the others come out. And I'll call the appliance guy when I get home." I considered this for a second. "I don't know an appliance guy. Do you?"

"Yep. McElroy Haynes. Best appliance guy around here. I'll get you his number before you go."

A click came from the direction of the kitchen.

"That's the oven," she said. "Want me to put the brownies in?"

"No, thanks. I'll do it. Would you mind seeing if you can find Mr. Haynes' number?"

"I'm on it."

I slid the pan of brownies into the oven, and she returned with the phone number.

"He's kinda crotchety, but tell him I told you to call. And tell him I said he was the best in the business."

I smiled. "I could just offer him brownies. Along with his payment, of course."

"I doubt it'd do you a bit of good, but you can try. Besides, you can't give away all your brownies. You have to sell some at the Save-A-Buck."

Setting the timer on my phone to alert me in twenty minutes, I told Myra I'd be back with the other pan soon.

I hurried back across the yards to my house to get the next batch of brownies underway but stopped short when I noticed a blue pickup truck parked in my driveway. I slowed my pace and approached cautiously.

The truck had Tennessee tags. There was no one inside it, and I'd left my door unlocked.

I didn't want to overreact. I still had a lot of friends in Tennessee. Maybe it was one of them. Besides, there was no indication that the person was actually inside my house. He— or she—could be a salesperson going door to door and had chosen my driveway as a good parking spot.

Thinking it best to err on the side of caution, I opened the door slightly. "Hello?"

"Hello."

That voice chilled my blood. It belonged to Todd Martin, my ex-husband.

CHAPTER TWO

I froze. I hadn't heard that voice in nearly seven years, but it chilled me to the bone. I began to hyperventilate and backed away from the door.

"Come here! Daphne, I'm not going to hurt you."

I had to move, had to get away. But then Todd burst through the door and grabbed my shoulders.

"P-please let me go. I-I'm sorry...for what you've been through."

He pulled me to his rock-hard chest in a constricting hug. "None of that matters. I've had a lot of time to think. And I'm different. I've changed. I still love you."

"L-let me go. Please."

"Not until you agree to come inside and talk with me. You owe me that after what you put me through, don't you think?"

I nodded. "Whatever...whatever you say."

"There's no reason to be afraid of me, Daph. I know I scared you before—and that cost me dearly—but I've forgiven you for having me put in prison."

My throat was constricted, my nose was running, and tears were coursing down my cheeks. I could barely breathe. I nodded again.

Todd loosened his grip. "Look at me."

I didn't want to. I'd been trying for years to forget that face...those merciless, accusing hazel eyes...the thin lips always ready to curl into a snarl or a smirk.

"I said, look at me." He shook me slightly, and I raised my eyes. "That's better. Do you see how much I love you? Can't you read it on my face?"

I nodded.

He wiped my tears away with his thumbs. "Don't cry. I'm here now." He ran his hands over my hair and then pressed me against his chest again. "I'd forgotten how good it felt to hold my wife."

"W-why don't I…make us some coffee?"

"All right. That'd be great."

He let me go but put me in front of him so I'd have to go inside the house. I went into the kitchen, and he followed so closely that if I'd stopped abruptly, he'd have stepped on my heels. If I was going to get away, it was going to be by using my wits rather than my strength. That much hadn't changed.

"I still buy that French roast coffee you always liked," I said.

Todd chuckled, took my shoulders, and kissed the back of my head. "You've got a nice place here. At least, what I've seen of it so far. How's the job market?"

"Pretty good, I guess."

He pulled out a kitchen chair and lowered his tall, bulky frame into it. "How's this…baking…thing going?"

"Fine." I busied myself with the coffee pot, waiting for him to become complacent.

"Your mom thinks you need to go back into secretarial work, but I don't see why you couldn't do both."

My mom… I clenched my teeth.

"Where's your bathroom?" he asked.

Thank God. "It's down the hall and to your left."

KILLER WEDDING CAKE · 21

"Be right back." He smiled, winked, and strode toward the bathroom.

As soon as I heard the door shut, I ran out the side door, through the backyard, and into Myra's house. I never even stopped to knock. I closed her door behind me and locked it. Then I sank to the floor and buried my face in my hands.

"Lord, have mercy! What's the matter?" Myra came and put her arms around me. "Tell me what's wrong."

I couldn't. All I could do was sit there and sob.

"Aw, hon. Everything'll be all right." She hugged me close. "Was it McElroy? Did you call him, and he was mean to you? If he was, I'll light into him like a fox on a June bug."

I shook my head. "It's Todd."

"Who? Todd?" It seemed to take a few seconds for her to remember who he was. "Wait, the killer? That Todd?"

I nodded. Even though he hadn't actually killed me— obviously—that's how Myra chose to refer to him.

"What about him?"

"He's at my house."

"Oh, dear sweet Jesus. I'm calling the police." She stood. "Get over there, Bruno, and protect her. Daphne, honey, are you hurt? Do I need to have them send an ambulance too?"

"No. Just the police."

Dutifully, Bruno came and took his mistress's place at my side. He anxiously pranced on his tiny feet before half climbing up my side to lick the salty tears off my face.

"Forgive me for saying so, but I don't think you'd be much protection against Todd Martin," I said to Bruno softly.

He didn't seem to take any offense to that and crawled into my lap. He wasn't much in the way of protection, but he was an old hand at offering comfort.

Myra returned from wherever she'd been using the phone. "They're on their way. I asked for McAfee because he's the most intimidating."

I knew the whole truth. She'd asked for McAfee because, as she'd told him on more than one occasion, he reminded her of that "gorgeous Shemar Moore from Criminal Minds." He was intimidating, though. He certainly had Bruno beat by a longshot.

"Did you happen to peep outside?" I asked. "Is there still a blue truck in my driveway?"

"I did, and there is."

"I just want him to leave."

She held out her hand. "Here. Get up and sit with me on the couch."

I took her hand, cradled Bruno with the other one, and got up. I sat on the sofa, still feeling somewhat dazed.

"I knew he was getting out of prison soon, but I just hadn't given it any serious thought."

"Well, that's understandable," she said. "You've had your upcoming wedding on your mind. You're thinking about your future, not the past."

"True. And I never dreamed he'd come here looking for me."

"Are you sure he didn't hurt you?" Myra gingerly lifted my wrist so she could examine my arm.

"I'm fine...physically."

"Did he threaten you?"

"Actually, no. He said he loved me and that he'd forgiven me for having him put in prison."

She let out a low growl that startled Bruno. "He put his own self in prison! Dirty rat!"

The little dog began to bark.

"You hush up," she told him. "Save your strength in case the rat gets here before Officer McAfee does."

The timer on my phone went off.

"I'll get the brownies." I turned off the alarm. I went into the kitchen, washed my hands, and put on the oven mitt that was designed to look like a large strawberry. As I was taking the brownies out of the oven, the doorbell rang, followed by Bruno's yapping.

"Thank the good Lord you're here!" Myra exclaimed. "We're in mortal fear for our lives! Hush up, Bruno! We've been rescued."

If I were to tell you that Myra Jenkins didn't have a dramatic streak a mile wide, I'd be lying.

I put the pan on a wire rack to allow the brownies to cool before joining Myra and the officer in the living room. Officer McAfee looked relieved to see me. She was holding to his right arm for dear life.

"Ms. Martin, what's going on?" He gently disengaged himself from her grasp and took out a notepad and pen.

I explained that my former husband had been in prison for assault with a deadly weapon. "Earlier today, my oven went out, so I came over here to use Myra's oven to bake a pan of brownies."

"Don't they smell good?" she asked McAfee.

"Yes, ma'am. Please continue, Ms. Martin."

"I set the timer on my phone and went back to my house with the intention of mixing up the second batch of brownies I need to make today. The blue pickup truck with Tennessee tags was in my driveway. There was no one in the truck, and

I'd left my door unlocked so I was afraid that the person was in my house."

"And this person was your ex-husband?"

"Yes!" Myra answered. "And he's this big old bear of a man. I don't know how on earth Daphne got away from him."

Officer McAfee frowned and stopped writing. "When did you see the man, Ms. Jenkins?"

"Oh, I didn't. But when Daphne got here the second time, she was scared half to death. I don't think some scrawny little old thing could scare her, do you?"

He pinched the bridge of his nose and took a deep breath. "Ms. Martin, what did you do upon realizing that the driver of the truck might be in your residence?"

"I called out, and he answered me. Before I could run, he came out of the house and grabbed me."

"Did he assault you?"

"No, I wouldn't say that. But, given our history, I was frightened."

"He's done tried to kill her once," Myra said. "Who's to say he's not here to try again?"

"I understand that, Ms. Jenkins." McAfee stepped out onto the porch and looked toward my house. "The truck is gone. Why don't we walk over to your house and make sure there's no one there and see if anything is missing?"

"All right," I said.

"Let me put Bruno in his crate before we go."

"Ms. Jenkins, as a matter of safety, I believe it would be best if you stay here for the moment."

"You'll come back and let me know what's going on, won't you?" she asked. "I harbored Daphne, gave her sanctuary or whatever you call it. That killer might be after me now too."

"I'll check back on you, Ms. Jenkins."

As McAfee and I walked across the yards, he offered me his arm. "Here. You seem a tad unsteady."

"I am." I gratefully took his arm. "If I hadn't frozen at the sound of his voice... But it was the last thing I was ever expecting to hear again, especially in such close proximity."

"Did the man give you any indication that he was out for revenge?"

"No. In fact, he said he forgave me for having him put in prison."

"Did he ask if you'd forgiven him for taking a shot at you?" he asked.

"No, sir."

"That was a joke, Ms. Martin."

"Oh. Yeah."

He patted my hand, which was probably cutting the circulation off his upper arm. "It'll be okay."

"Unless it isn't."

"I'm here now. After we're done going through your house, we're going to report back to Ms. Jenkins, of course." Officer McAfee shook his head. "And after that, we're going to the station so you can see the magistrate for an emergency order of protection."

"Will this order be printed on an iron shield or a Kevlar vest? If it's not, I'm not sure how it'll stop a bullet."

"If he returns, you call the station, and somebody will be here as soon as possible."

I nodded and murmured my thanks, but I still didn't feel terribly reassured.

We got to my carport, and I released his arm. I didn't want to restrict him in any way in case he might need to draw his gun or throw a punch or whatever. Since Todd's truck was gone and I hadn't seen anyone else around, I didn't think that would be an issue. But it was certainly better to have the officer unencumbered if necessary.

"Anything out here look amiss?" he asked.

"No."

"All right. I'm going in first. You stay close behind me."

He didn't need to worry on that account.

"Tell me if you see anything that looks strange or out of place."

"Okay, I will."

We walked through the kitchen, living room, down the hall, into the bathroom, and finally into both bedrooms. We checked all the closets. Nothing seemed to be stolen or out of order, and I said so to McAfee.

"Get your purse and your keys and lock up," he said. "I'm going back to reassure Ms. Jenkins that everything is okay, get my car, and then I'll be back. You can follow me to the station, and I'll take you in to see the magistrate."

"All right. Please tell Myra that I'll get the brownies as soon as I get back."

"I think those should be the least of your worries at the moment, Ms. Martin, but I'll let her know."

I thanked him again, and he left through the front door.

When I went to the kitchen to get my purse and keys from the hook near the side door, I noticed a piece of paper on the table. I regarded it as I might a dead mouse or some other "gift" left by Sparrow—it was unpleasant, but I needed to deal with it and get it out of my house.

I felt a twinge of morbid curiosity as I reached for the letter. If the letter contained a threat, it might help persuade the magistrate to award me the protection order, and that made me feel better about wanting to know what Todd had said.

Daphne:

I do still love you, and I think we could still work things out. You're not married yet, so it's not too late. I miss seeing my granny's ring on your finger. Will you give me another chance?

Todd

Another chance to what? Kill me? I sighed.

The letter probably wouldn't be helpful. There wasn't anything threatening in it. Still, I shuddered as I wadded the paper up into a ball and flung it into the trash can.

All these years, and I hadn't heard a word from Todd. Not a note, not a call, not a Christmas card. Now all of a sudden, he loved me and wanted to work things out? What was he up to?

CHAPTER THREE

I started when Officer McAfee knocked on the door to tell me he was ready to go to the magistrate's office. How long would it be before my heart stopped racing and I quit being freaked out by every sudden noise?

"Are you all right to drive?" he asked. "You still appear to be pretty shaken up."

"I found a note that Todd left on the kitchen table for me. I just hate that he had the run of my house like he did."

"Let me see the letter." He held out his hand.

"I…um…I threw it away."

"Did he make any threats in this letter?"

I shook my head.

"And you're sure nothing was taken?"

"I'm fairly sure."

"If you realize something is missing later on, give us a call at the sheriff's office." He gazed around the room as if reassuring himself that nothing appeared to be damaged.

"All right. Can we go now? I'd like to get this over with."

"Of course. I'll lead the way. If you need to stop for any reason, blink your headlights."

* * *

The magistrate's office was right beside the jail. McAfee parked, got out of his cruiser, and motioned for me to take the empty space beside him. I pulled my red Mini-Cooper into the spot.

Before I could grab my purse from the passenger seat, he had come around and opened the driver's side door. He kept one hand on my shoulder as he looked around—I assumed he was making sure there was no one suspicious lurking outside the building. Maybe he was looking for a blue pickup truck with Tennessee tags.

That he was being so cautious made me both glad and apprehensive. Would he take it the wrong way if I asked him to come back to my house and spend the night? Would Ben? He was my first choice of overnight protector, but he was out of town.

"I'm scared," I said.

He looked down at me then, and I could see the compassion in his eyes. "I know. You shouldn't be alone this evening."

Had he read my mind?

"Is there someone you could stay with? I wouldn't mind going back with you to pack a bag."

"I'll call my sister." I was already thinking of a way to make my overnight visit plausible to Lucas and Leslie. My oven wasn't working, and I needed to stay with them in order to get the baking done for the Save-A-Buck. The kids would be happy to help me in the kitchen, and they'd keep my mind off of Todd. Hopefully, tomorrow, my ex would be back in Tennessee and everything would be all right.

The magistrate was a short, stout woman with tightly curled brown hair. She wore a navy pantsuit and black loafers. She was looking pretty stern until she spotted Officer McAfee, and then her face broke into a smile.

"Well, hi there, handsome. Who's this you've brought me?"

He explained how my ex-husband had been incarcerated in Tennessee for assault with a deadly weapon after he'd shot at me and missed. "He's out of prison now—I checked it out on the way here and he was released—"

It had never crossed my mind that Todd might've escaped.

"He paid Ms. Martin a visit today," he continued. "She was next door at a neighbor's house, and when she returned, she found Mr. Martin inside her home."

The magistrate arched a brow at me. "You should never leave your doors unlocked, even when you're only running out for a moment."

"I know," I said softly. I felt like saying, Lesson learned, lady. Can we move this thing along?

Her face softened as she looked at McAfee again. "Did he threaten her?"

"No, but given the fact that his incarceration was due to an apparent attempt on Ms. Martin's life, I think an emergency protective order should be issued." He smiled. "Don't you?"

"I'll defer to your judgment."

I was confident that smile sealed the deal.

The magistrate explained to me that the emergency protective order was an ex parte order, meaning that Todd was not present nor did he have to be notified beforehand of the issuance. The order would grant me protection for the next three days and was intended to stop any contact Todd had with me or my family or any household members.

"To get a regular order of protection, you'll need to go before a judge," the magistrate told me.

"Hopefully, Todd will be gone before that becomes necessary," I said.

"If he contacts you or returns to your home, inform him that you have an emergency order of protection against him. If he continues to harass you or refuses to leave, call the sheriff's department immediately."

"Thank you. I will."

Officer McAfee walked me back to my car. I was grateful that he did, but I thought that not even Todd was dumb enough to approach me so close to a jail.

"I'll follow you back to your house to make sure Mr. Martin hasn't returned."

"Thanks." I got into the car, pulled out of the parking lot, and called Violet to ask if I could stay at her house this evening. My call went straight to voicemail.

"Hey, Vi. I'm calling to see if I could stay at your house tonight. My oven is on the fritz, and I have some baking to do." I debated on whether or not to tell her the whole truth. I plunged ahead. "And that's not all. Todd's in town. He came to my house and scared the crap out of me. Guess who gave him my address? Mom. Can you believe that? Oh, well. Call me."

I was thinking of what I needed to pack, including all the ingredients I'd need for my baking. Once I was ready to leave, I'd try to call Violet again. If, for some reason, I couldn't crash there, maybe I could stay with Myra. I made a mental note to get the brownies cut and boxed before I packed my bag.

I pulled into my driveway and wasn't as surprised as many people might've been to find China York sitting on my carport with a double-barreled shotgun on her lap.

McAfee pulled in behind me.

"China, put that thing away!" I said under my breath as I got out of the car. "I take it you heard."

"Yep. Came over the police scanner." She made no attempt to hide the gun. "They didn't name names, but how many people in Brea Ridge have an ex-husband who tried to kill her? I didn't jump to the wrong conclusion, did I?"

"You sure didn't." I looked back toward McAfee.

He strode over and plucked the shotgun off China's lap. "Is that a Winchester 21, Ms. York?"

She nodded once. "It was one of my daddy's guns."

"Nice." Officer McAfee opened the gun, removed the shells, and put them into his shirt pocket.

"How am I supposed to help protect Daphne with an empty gun?"

He grinned. "You wouldn't want to take a man's job away from him, would you, Ms. York?"

"No, but you won't be hanging around. Or will you?"

"I'm afraid not. But just seeing you with that shotgun is enough to make most men pause." He handed the gun back to China. "You ever shot that thing?"

"Yes, indeed."

"Recoil knock you down?"

She tightened her mouth. "No. Give me back them shells, and I'll show you how well I can shoot."

"Some other time maybe." McAfee laughed and turned to me. "Will you be all right if I head back to the station?"

"I will."

He left with instructions for me to call immediately should Todd return.

"Come on in, and I'll give you a glass of iced tea," I said to China.

She stood and dusted off the seat of her jeans. "I'll take you up on that."

I unlocked the door, and we went inside.

China looked around appraisingly before placing the shotgun in the corner by the door. "Don't worry. I have two more shells in my pocket. Want me to go ahead and reload?"

I shook my head. What if Todd should come back, kick open the door, and have a loaded shotgun right there handy? He might kill us both.

"Doesn't appear that he did any damage to your place."

"He didn't, at least, not that I've been able to tell yet. He left me a note, but I threw it in the trash."

"Let me guess. He loves you and wants you back."

"How'd you know?" I asked.

"Stands to reason. He just got out of prison. He has no idea what to do next. Maybe he thinks that since you've started a new life here, he can just be part of that."

"Then, boy, has he got another think coming."

China chuckled. "Did they give you a restraining order?"

I nodded. "They're calling it an emergency order of protection, and it's only good for three days. But hopefully Todd will be long gone before those three days are up, and I won't have to go before a judge and go through all of that rigmarole."

"Well, I hope so, hon. But don't get your hopes up too high."

"Why not?"

"What else has Todd Martin got?" she asked.

I hadn't thought of that.

"And, I'm sorry to say so, but those restraining orders are about as good as the paper they're written on. That's why I'm loaning you my shotgun."

"Oh, no, China." My eyes widened. "I wouldn't have the first idea of how to use that thing."

"You pick it up, point it, and shoot. Hopefully, all you'd have to do is threaten him. But I can show you how to use it in case you need to."

"I'll be fine," I insisted. "I'm planning to stay with Violet, Jason, and the kids tonight. Todd wouldn't dare do anything there."

"Has Jason got a gun?"

I had no idea. "Probably."

"Make sure before you leave here. I've got a couple of smaller guns if you think you'd be more comfortable with a pistol. The thing about a pistol is that you've got to be a fair to middling shot to make it count. And when you're nervous, your aim is likely to be off. That's why—if it was just going to be you here by yourself—I thought you'd be better off with the shotgun."

"I…I sure do appreciate that."

Before I had to discuss my need—or lack thereof—of a gun any further, Violet called.

"Please excuse me, China. I need to speak with Violet for just a second." I answered the call. "Hi, there."

"I cannot believe the nerve of that big, overgrown jerk!"

I smiled slightly. "It's all right, Vi. I'm not hurt."

"I'm not talking about you! He came to our house!"

"He what?"

"He came to our house and said he wanted to get reacquainted with his niece and nephew," she said. "He said he had presents for them out in his truck and that he wanted to make sure it was all right with me and Jason if he gave the gifts to them."

"What did the kids say—or do?" I groaned. "Did they even know who he was?"

"Thank goodness they were at day camp and missed the whole ordeal."

"How did you get Todd to leave?"

"First off, I never undid the chain on the door. I told him—truthfully—that the kids weren't home but that I didn't think it was such a good idea for him to come back into their lives right now."

"What do you mean, come back into their lives?" I scoffed. "He was never in their lives to begin with."

"I know. But I was trying to be...I don't know. Diplomatic. But I know this much—he'd better stay away from my kids!"

"He will." I sighed. "Maybe I shouldn't spend the night with you guys after all."

"Of course, you're spending the night with us. I don't want you over there by yourself. What if the idiot decides to come back in the middle of the night? Who's going to protect you—that poor little one-eyed cat?"

She was right. Sparrow wasn't much of a guard cat. She'd likely dive under the bed at the merest hint of a commotion.

"But what if he returns to your house?"

"Then we'll call the police. Get your butt over here before I come and get you myself."

"I did get an emergency order of protection," I said. "That might make the police come out quicker if we do have to call them."

I ignored China's look of doubt.

"Please say you're coming and that you'll get here soon," Violet said. "And, as far as the kids go, we're sticking with your story about the oven."

"The story about the oven is true. Myra gave me the name of someone to call."

"Okay. Good. See you soon."

When I ended the call, China had one eye closed and was looking up at the ceiling. "Who'd Myra tell you to call about the oven—McElroy Haynes?"

"Yeah. Why?"

"He does know his way around appliances, but he's the hatefulest man this side of Red Onion."

Red Onion was a super-max state prison located in Wise County, Virginia. Now I wasn't sure I wanted Mr. Haynes anywhere near my oven, much less, me.

"Do you know of anybody else?"

"Not anybody as good as Haynes. But if he won't come out and fix your oven in a reasonable amount of time and at a reasonable price, give me a call. I'll see who else I can come up with."

"Want to go with me to Myra's to get the brownies I left there?"

"Sure." She grabbed the shotgun. "Let's go."

I locked the door, put my keys in the pocket of my jeans, and headed off after Annie Oakley. When we got to Myra's house, I knocked this time rather than barging right in. I needed to apologize for my earlier behavior.

Myra opened the door. "Lord, have mercy! Are you gonna kill me, China?"

"No, this is in case that old Todd has little enough sense to show his sorry face around here again."

"Oh, all right. Come on in then." She backed up and let us into the foyer. "Is that thing loaded?"

"Not at the moment. But we can change that if we have to." She propped the shotgun against the wall.

Bruno went over to sniff the weapon.

"I wouldn't do that, little bit," China said. "If that thing falls on you, it'll squash you flatter than a bug."

The dog apparently understood what she said because it scurried away.

"Thank you for all your help earlier," I said to Myra. "And please forgive me for just barging in here."

"Honey, that's okay. You were scared out of your mind."

"Yes, I was."

"What happened at the police station?"

I explained about the protection order and then joked about the fact that I nearly asked Officer McAfee to stay the night with me because I was so scared.

Myra put her hand on her chest. "Why didn't you? I'd have come over and helped him stand watch."

"I doubt Mark would've thought too much of that." Myra was dating private investigator Mark Thompson.

"What Mark don't know won't hurt him. Now Ben might be another story."

"Will you two just hush?" China teased. "I'm the single lady around here. And I can shoot. If anybody needs to help Officer Good-lookin' stand guard, it's me."

We all laughed. I went into the kitchen and cut each of us a brownie.

"We might as well enjoy this batch," I said. "I'll give you guys some of them, and I'll take the rest to Violet's house with me. I'm going to stay there tonight so I can catch up on my baking."

"To catch up on your baking or because you're afraid Todd'll come back?" Myra asked.

"Both," I said.

CHAPTER FOUR

On the drive to Violet's house, I called Ben. The call went to voicemail—as I'd expected, since he was in Asheville, North Carolina for some sort of newspaper conference. I left him a brief message telling him that my oven wasn't working and that I was going to spend the night at Vi's house to get caught up on my baking. I didn't tell him about Todd's visit. That was something one didn't just spill in a voicemail message.

When I got to my sister's house, she came out and carried in my overnight bag so I could wrestle the box of baking supplies from the car. She put the bag in the guest room and then returned to the kitchen.

"What time will Lucas and Leslie be home?" I asked.

She glanced at the clock which hung on the wall over the sink. "They should be here in half an hour or so."

"Good. I'm looking forward to seeing them. Not that I'm not happy to see you. It's just that their energy will be a breath of fresh air for me after the day I've had."

"Sit down and talk a minute." Violet went over to the kitchen table. "Would you like something to drink?"

"No, I'm fine." Still, I joined her at the table.

"Are you all right?"

I nodded. "Sure."

"Are you really? I know what a shock seeing Todd must've been for you. It was a shock for me!"

"It was. I was caught so off guard." I looked down at the wood grain of the table and traced a line with my fingertip. "I guess that somewhere buried deep in my subconscious, I knew Todd's sentence was about up. But I never thought he'd come here."

"And I never thought he'd come here. He said he wanted to get to know Leslie and Lucas again." She blew out a breath. "Hello? He never knew them in the first place. He never wanted anything to do with them before."

"I know. I'm sorry he came to your house. He shouldn't have. I guess it was another tool in his arsenal to get to me."

"I spoke with Jason right after I made Todd leave. He said he was going to call the prison and see if coming here to Brea Ridge was in violation of any terms of Todd's parole. He did cross the state border after all."

I raised my head. "Have you heard back from him?"

"Not yet. But he'll let us know what he finds out as soon as he knows something."

"I cannot believe Mom gave him my address!" I said. "Oh, wait. Yes, I can. It's Mom. She thought I'd driven him to take a shot at me, remember?"

"I don't think she truly believed that, Daph. She was just trying to give Todd the benefit of the doubt. I'll call her later and get her side of the story."

"Better you than me."

We heard the bus pull up outside.

"That's the church bus dropping off the kids," Violet said.

Seconds later, the twin tornadoes tore through the kitchen.

"I'm starving!" Lucas called before he saw that I was there.

"Aunt Daphne!" Leslie launched herself into my arms.

After we'd hugged, Lucas put his arms around me and tried to pick me up. He succeeded in knocking me slightly off balance.

"It won't be long," I told him. "You're getting really strong."

"I know. I've been lifting weights."

"I can tell."

"What're you doing here?" Leslie asked.

"My oven is on the fritz, so I'm spending the night here to catch up on my baking…if that's all right with you guys."

They both cheered.

"Let me fix you a snack, and then you'll need to be quiet while Aunt Daphne calls the repairman," Violet said.

"Oh, yeah. I'd forgotten about that." I got out my cell phone and the number Myra had given me while my sister gave each of the children some apple slices and tablespoon of peanut butter.

I punched in Mr. Haynes' number. Within seconds, a voice croaked, "Yeah."

"Mr. Haynes?"

"Yeah!"

"My name is Daphne Martin, and I'd like you to take a look at my oven. Myra Jenkins gave me your number. She says you're the best around."

"Address?"

I gave him my address.

"Be there at ten o'clock tomorrow morning. If you ain't there, I'll leave. Won't be back either."

"Oh, I'll be there," I said. "I'll look forward to seeing you."

Mr. Haynes hung up.

"What a sweetheart." I put my phone away and told the kids how brusque the man had been. Then the three of us had a blast pretending that McElroy Haynes was "the oven troll" and that he'd make me prepare cookies or a cake or some other baked goods for him once a week for the rest of my life in order to keep my oven in working order.

Violet even joined in the fun, suggesting that Mr. Haynes wasn't a troll but rather an elf. "Maybe he lives in an elm tree and makes cookies himself."

Lucas and Leslie preferred him to be a troll. I agreed. Especially after hearing him speak. Elves had a nicer predisposition than trolls, right?

"Before I dive into my baking, what were you planning to make for dinner?" I asked Violet.

"I hadn't really given it much thought yet."

"Then, since I'm commandeering your oven, why don't you let me order pizza and breadsticks?"

"That sounds good," she said. "We'll call it in, and I'll have Jason pick it up on the way."

"What're you baking, Aunt Daphne?" Leslie asked.

"Brownies and cookies. Hopefully, I'll have my oven back in time to use it to bake my cakes tomorrow."

"Brownies, eh? Somebody'll need to taste test those for sure," Lucas said.

"Lucas." His mother gave him a half serious frown.

"No, he's absolutely right." I neglected to tell him before dinner that I already had some set aside for the family. "I can't take brownies to the Save-A-Buck unless they've been through the quality control test. My reputation is on the line here."

"Exactly." He gave me a smug smile. "She's never used your oven before, Mom, and they all heat differently."

I decided then and there that he was going to grow up to be either a politician or a lawyer. Possibly both.

Once we'd gotten the pizza order all squared away, I got started on my second batch of brownies of the day. I should've been done with them hours ago. And about half the cookies too, for that matter. But the day hadn't turned out as I'd expected in the least.

Leslie was delighted to be able to help mix up the chocolate chip cookie dough while the brownies were baking. She had a real love of baking and cake decorating too. She'd even won first place in the junior category at a recent cake decorating competition held here in Brea Ridge.

Todd and the drama that had followed him into town seemed like it was miles away. For a while anyway.

* * *

When Jason got home, he put the pizza and breadstick boxes on the kitchen table, kissed his wife and kids, and then gave me a hug.

"Are you okay?" he asked.

I nodded. "I'm fine. Or at least, I will be."

"Yeah, the guy is coming to fix her oven at ten in the morning," Leslie said.

"But if she's not there when he gets there, he's leaving," Lucas chimed in. "And he ain't coming back."

I laughed. "They know all about it."

"It sounds like it." Jason lowered his voice. "We're here for you. You know that."

"I appreciate that."

"Yeah, Aunt Daphne. You can use our oven anytime," said Leslie.

Jason winked. He was a good-looking guy—red hair, blue eyes. When he and Violet were dating, I'd teased him by calling him Richie Cunningham. In turn, he'd called me Joanie. And he'd always treated me like a sister. Vi and I were both lucky to have him. It went without saying how fortunate the kids were to have him for a dad.

For the next few hours, we baked, ate pizza, and watched a movie. Lucas and Leslie got to taste test the brownies and cookies, but they were finally able to wind down and go to bed. I was cleaning the kitchen when Jason and Violet came in and sat at the table.

"You don't have to leave the place spotless, you know," Violet said. "I mean, you've cleaned up after yourself and moved into spring cleaning territory."

"I know. It's just that you guys did me a huge favor, and I'm trying to pay you back."

"It has nothing to do with the fact that you're afraid to let your mind wander?" Jason asked. "I've experienced the need to throw myself into mindless tasks in order to avoid thinking about something unpleasant."

"That might be a small part of it."

"Come sit down," Violet said.

I pulled out a chair and dropped into it. I immediately felt weary and tired.

"You're exhausted," she said. "You should go to bed."

"I will…soon."

"Have you told Ben about Todd coming to town?" Jason asked.

"No. He's at a conference." I glanced up at the clock. "Actually, he's probably on his way home now. I tried to call him earlier, and my call went to voicemail. I couldn't tell him something like that in a message, so I just told him my oven wasn't working and that I was spending the night here."

"I called the prison and left a message with the warden's secretary, but I haven't heard back yet," Jason said. "I think you should stay here—or if not here, with someone—until we're sure Todd has left town. You shouldn't be home alone."

"I'll be fine," I insisted. "I'll keep my doors locked, and I'll stay inside...especially if I hear anyone outside."

"I'm worried about how Ben will react to the news of Todd showing up so close to your wedding day," Violet said. "I mean, there's history there. And even though you had nothing to do with Todd's coming here, there's bound to be some hurt feelings on Ben's part."

I merely nodded. I didn't need to be reminded of the fact that I'd broken up with Ben—my high school sweetheart—to date the abusive monster who'd almost taken my life. Surely, Ben had to know that I'd never do anything to jeopardize our relationship...at least, not anymore. I sighed and closed my eyes.

Violet was right. This was going to be tough for Ben. I really needed to talk with him and get this mess out in the open before someone else told him about it. He had a lot of connections on the police force. It would be terrible if one of the officers mentioned Todd's coming to Brea Ridge and I hadn't already told him. He might jump to the wrong conclusion about why I was keeping it from him.

I started at the touch of Violet's hand on mine.

"Daph, go on to bed."

"Okay."

"If you need anything, we're here," Jason said.

"Thanks." I went to the guest room, sat on the side of the bed, and called Ben. This time, he picked up.

"Hey, beautiful. I was getting ready to call you. How's the baking going?"

"I'm finished for the night. I'm really tired."

"Tired from baking or from playing with the twins?"

I chuckled. "Both."

"Have you spoken with someone about the oven?"

"Yes. McElroy Haynes is going to be at my house in the morning at ten o'clock to look at it." I hesitated. "There's something else I need to tell you."

"Is this news as dreadful as the tone of your voice is indicating it is?"

"Even worse. I got a surprise visit from Todd today."

There was a long silence. Finally, Ben said, "So he's out."

"Yes."

"Are you okay?"

"Yes." I forced a note of intrepidness into my voice. "He didn't hurt me. I ran next door, and Myra called the police. Officer McAfee took me to the magistrate, and I was awarded an emergency protection order."

"Did he threaten you?" Ben asked.

"No. The order was granted based on the fact that his trying to kill me is what put him in prison."

"What did he want then?" There was an edge to his voice.

"I'm not sure," I said. "He acts like he wants to be back in everybody's life—he even came here to Violet's house and said he wanted to see the kids. Of course, Vi sent him packing. She was furious."

"I can imagine."

"I really don't know what he's doing here, Ben. But I'll feel a lot better once he's gone." I was desperate for him to know how much I meant those words.

"You and me both."

CHAPTER FIVE

I slept surprisingly well and got up early the next morning to make breakfast. Jason stumbled into the kitchen in his pajama bottoms while I was making pancakes and was thrilled to find that I'd already made coffee.

"You're a godsend," he said.

I smiled. "Making breakfast is the least I could do. How do you like your eggs?"

"Anyway you want to make them is fine with me." He poured his coffee and sat down at the table with the newspaper. "Are you all right this morning? You don't have to be in such a hurry to go back home, you know."

"I know." I flipped the pancakes. "Funny, huh? How I thought I was through running from that man?"

"You are through," Jason said. "He's never going to bother you again."

I wished I could be sure.

The sound of smaller feet shuffling into the room alerted me that either Lucas or Leslie was up.

"Pancakes! Yes!"

"Good morning, Lucas," I said.

He wrapped his arms around my waist and pressed his face against my shoulder. He'd gotten taller since the last time he'd given me a hug like this.

"Have I told you how much I love having you stay here?" he asked. "You should just move in. It'd save you money in the long run."

"I'm getting married in a week and a half, remember?"

"Oh, yeah. Well, Ben wouldn't take up too much more room, would he?"

I laughed softly. "How about I just promise to keep coming over and making you food sometimes? And, of course, you and Leslie are always welcome to visit me."

"Sounds good," said Leslie. She then addressed her brother. "How about moving your big butt so I can see what Aunt Daphne is making?"

"Your butt's bigger than mine."

"Sit down, and I'll get you guys some milk," Jason said.

I grinned at my brother-in-law and hummed the first two lines ofMorning Has Broken.

He rolled his eyes and called to Violet that breakfast was almost ready. That roughly translated to, "Get in here! I can't handle these people by myself."

By the time I'd finished the pancakes, eggs, toast, and sausage, everyone was gathered around the table. The kids had called a truce, and Jason and Violet had ingested enough coffee to engage in intelligent conversation.

I could tell from the dark circles beneath Violet's eyes that she hadn't slept well. She probably wouldn't have admitted it to me, but I knew she was worried about Todd being in town—not just for my sake but for the sake of her children. She didn't want him anywhere near them, and neither did I.

The doorbell rang, and the three adults in the room became as still as statues. We exchanged glances as Jason stood.

"I've got this." He strode from the kitchen.

"What's up with Dad?" Lucas asked.

"It's not just Dad. Everybody seems freaked out," Leslie said. "Is there a killer on the loose or something?"

"No!" I forced out a laugh. "We just don't want to share our breakfast!"

Lucas nodded. "Makes sense to me."

Violet and I let out a collective breath when we heard Jason greeting Ben at the door. I quickly got him a plate. When the two men came into the kitchen, I embraced Ben. Tears pricked my eyes, and I held him tight.

He kissed me and whispered that everything was all right. I nodded but didn't let go yet.

"Can we eat now?" Lucas asked.

"Of course." I dragged myself away and discreetly wiped my eyes. "Ben, I've put you here beside me."

As we ate, Jason asked Ben a million and forty questions about the conference in Asheville.

"Did you bring us back anything?" Leslie asked.

Jason and Violet both protested her question, but Ben laughed.

"I didn't. I was stuck at the hotel the entire time. But maybe your Aunt Daphne and I can take you guys to Biltmore sometime this fall if it's okay with your parents."

This suggestion went over well with the kids. Jason and Violet would be all for it too, once they got over being embarrassed by Leslie's asking if Ben had brought them a souvenir. I looked at Leslie's question as a good thing—she felt comfortable enough to treat Ben like family.

Not long after the children went to get ready for day camp, Jason's cell phone rang. He walked into the living room to take the call. When he returned, he told us that it was the warden of the prison where Todd had been incarcerated who had called.

"I called and left a message yesterday," Jason explained to Ben. "I wanted to see if Todd's being in Virginia was in violation of his parole."

"And is it?" Violet asked hopefully.

Jason shook his head. "I'm afraid not. Since Todd served his full sentence, he isn't on parole. Still, if he doesn't comply with Daphne's emergency protection order, he'll be arrested."

"Don't worry, guys. I made it clear to Todd that I'm not interested in talking with him, and I don't think he'll bother me again." I resisted the urge to feel my nose to see if my lie had caused it to grow.

* * *

Myra rushed over as I was pulling into the driveway. I was relieved I didn't have to go inside alone.

"How'd it go last night?" she asked as I was getting my overnight bag out of the car. "Did you guys have any trouble?"

"Nope. Hopefully, Todd got the message and has gone back to Tennessee." I handed her my keys. "Would you mind unlocking the door?"

"I guess not."

I put the strap of the overnight bag over my shoulder and grabbed the cardboard box filled with smaller boxes of cookies and brownies. I pushed the car door closed with my hip and waited for her to open the door. She was certainly taking her time about it.

"These are kinda heavy," I said.

"I can imagine." She slowly unlocked the door and then jumped to the side as she pushed it open.

"What was that?"

"I was afraid he might be in there."

"And, what? You didn't want to be in the line of fire?"

"Well, no! Would you?"

She had me there. I went on into the house. Everything looked just as I'd left it the day before.

"The coast is clear!" I put my overnight bag and the box on the counter.

"Are you sure?" Myra came in cautiously, looking all around the kitchen before peeking into the living room and then making her way down the hall. She'd poke open doors with two fingers and hop aside like some Easter Bunny-turned-cop.

I wanted to yell, "Boo!" just to mess with her. But, frankly, I was afraid she'd pee on herself.

"Myra, why on earth do you think Todd is here? He didn't come back last night, did he?"

"Not that I know of, but how do we know he ever even left?"

"Because his truck was gone? Because Officer McAfee went through the entire house? And because after he left here, he went to Violet's house."

"Still, he could've stashed that truck somewhere, walked back here, and got inside," she said. "He might be waylaying us right this very second in some little cranny. He could jump out of a closet or something and get us both."

"How could that be possible?"

"Oh, honey."

When Myra Jenkins started a story with oh, honey, it was time to get comfortable because whatever she was about to say might take a while. Her tales were never boring, though.

"One time when Carl Junior was in high school," she continued, "one of his friends was babysitting. I believe her name was Jenny. Anyhow, after she put the young 'uns to bed, somebody called her and told her she'd better check on them."

I frowned. "That sounds like a movie to me."

"Don't it though? So poor little Jenny thought it was somebody just messing with her. But they called again and said she'd better check on the young 'uns. Well, she checked on them, and they were fine."

"Let me guess," I said. "The police finally traced the call, and it was coming from inside the house?"

"No." She scrunched up her nose. "Why would it be coming from inside the house—unless it was one of the kids playing a trick on her? It turned out to be old Con Jackson who lived across the street from where Jenny was babysitting. He could see her through the window and didn't think she was doing a good enough job."

"What does that have to do with somebody being in your house without your knowing it?"

"Well, he was watching her, and that was almost as bad," Myra said. "Wasn't it?"

"I guess so."

"I bet there have been cases where people hid in a house without the owners knowing, though. Like what you said about somebody calling inside the house. What was that about?"

I waved my hand. "It was nothing. I was getting ahead of myself."

"Oh." She looked around one more time before she pulled out a chair and sat down. "I don't think he's in here."

"I don't think he is either. Would you like some coffee?"

"No. I'm all right," she said. "Did you get a hold of McElroy?"

"I did. He's supposed to be here at ten."

Myra wrinkled her forehead as she looked down at the table. "Do you kinda wonder what he has to say?"

"Of course. I hope you're right about it only being the heating element. That shouldn't be too hard or too expensive to fix."

"I don't mean McElroy. I mean Todd."

I sank into the chair across from her. "Yeah. I guess so. I don't know what would possibly possess him to come here."

"You said he told you he still loved you."

"He did." I shook my head. "But I don't believe Todd Martin ever loved me. Or anybody besides himself, for that matter. It has to be one of two things—either he wants something he believes I took from him, or he wants to ruin my relationship with Ben."

"If he can't have you, nobody can?" She raised her eyes and gave me a wry smile. "Reminds me of the boy who said if I went to prom with Carl instead of him that he'd die."

"What happened?"

"He died."

My jaw dropped. "Oh, my gosh!"

"Yep. It was fifty years later. But sure enough, he died."

We both burst out laughing.

"Thanks," I said. "I needed that."

The front doorbell rang.

"Huh." Myra looked up at the clock. "McElroy's early."

I went to the door. Instead of a scruffy old handyman, Officer McAfee was standing there.

"Ms. Martin." He nodded once. "May I come in please?"

"Of course. Come on into the kitchen." I led the way. "Would you like some coffee?"

"No, thank you."

"Well, hi, there! Did you come to protect us?" Myra placed a hand on her chest. "I know I'll feel safer with you here."

"Um...no, ma'am. That's not exactly why I'm here."

I looked up into his big brown eyes and knew something bad had happened. "What is it?"

"Could we speak privately?"

"Please feel free to say anything you need to say in front of Myra." This was Brea Ridge. If she didn't hear it from the horse's mouth, she'd hear it somewhere else within half an hour. At least this way, she could help keep the facts straight.

"It's your ex-husband. A man matching his description—and who registered at a nearby hotel under the name Todd Martin—was found dead this morning in his room."

I stumbled slightly, and Officer McAfee caught me by the shoulders and eased me into the chair I'd vacated to answer the door. "D-do you know...what happened?"

"He was shot. At close range." He stooped in front of me. "I'm sorry to do this, but I need you to come with me to identify the body."

CHAPTER SIX

Myra had promised to wait for McElroy Haynes and to feed Sparrow. I'd intended to feed the cat as soon as I got home but had failed to do so before Officer McAfee came calling. It was easier to think about mundane things like that while I rode in the police cruiser than to acknowledge the fact that I was on my way to the morgue to identify the body of my ex-husband.

I looked down at my hands and realized how tightly they were clenched. I opened them and saw the imprints of my fingernails on my palms.

"You all right over there?" McAfee asked.

"No," I said. "Not really."

"Talk to me."

I'd been interrogated by Officer McAfee during a murder investigation not too long ago. My ex-husband had arrived in town yesterday and was dead today under mysterious circumstances. And though I'd done nothing wrong, I wasn't sure this man was my best option in the confidante department.

"I'm just nervous." I fiddled with the zipper on my purse. "Is there any chance the person in the morgue could be someone other than Todd?"

"It could be. That's why I'm taking you to identify the body." He glanced over at me. "Just between us, are you hoping that it is him or not?"

"I hope it isn't! That man was my husband once."

"Still have feelings for him then?"

McAfee was acting all casual, but I knew that police officers—and this one in particular—were seldom casual.

"No, I don't still have feelings for him. But that doesn't mean I hope someone gunned him down in his hotel room just as he was trying to rebuild his life. I wish the best for Todd, just as I hope he wishes the best for me."

"Gee, that's awfully magnanimous of you, especially given the fact that the guy scared you so badly yesterday that you had to get an emergency order of protection."

"I wanted Todd to leave me alone. I didn't want something bad to happen to him. I honestly hope no harm has come to him and the body in the morgue belongs to somebody else."

"Really? I mean, you can be straight up with me, Daphne—this conversation isn't being recorded or anything." He braked at a stop sign and turned fully in my direction. "After what that man put you through. I mean, he took a shot at you—could've killed you—you don't wish him any harm?"

I blew out a breath before meeting McAfee's eyes. "No, sir, I don't. I only want to live my life in peace."

"Huh." He checked to make sure no traffic was coming in either direction and then pulled out. "You're a better person than I am. I don't think I'd feel so warm and fuzzy about someone who'd taken a shot at me."

"Todd and I were married. We had some good times, at least, at the early part of our marriage." I tried to recall some of those good times, but for the life of me, I couldn't get any of those memories to surface. All I could think about was Todd in my kitchen yesterday, his face inches from mine, his strong hands close enough to be able to wrap them around my throat.

* * *

Officer McAfee's strong right arm steadied me as he led me out of the morgue. I'd nearly fainted when I saw Todd's body. The things that went through my mind as I stared down at the dead man that I'd once loved so many years ago, the man that I didn't love anymore.

I felt guilty for no longer loving him and regretted ever loving him in the first place. I was sorry that the happiest he'd ever been—as far as I knew—was when he'd played football in college. I hated that his life had ended so soon and so tragically.

I lamented the fact that Todd had spent seven years of his life in prison—and, for the first time ever, I felt partially responsible for that. Yes, he was abusive and controlling and downright mean sometimes, but if I'd never married him, he wouldn't have shot at me and been hauled off to jail.

Racking my brain, I tried to remember something good about the man who lay on that cold metal slab with three bullet wounds in his upper torso. There had been fun times— tender moments, shared laughter. But, for the life of me, I couldn't recall a single incident as I stared down at Todd's ashen face.

After I made the positive identification, McAfee led me to the lobby where I was relieved to see Ben waiting for me. Actually, relieved was an understatement.

He held out his arms, and I practically collapsed into them. He gently sat me down onto one of the vinyl seats, and he sat on the chair next to me.

"It's all right," he whispered, stroking my hair. "Everything's okay."

I nodded. I wasn't weeping, but I was cold. In fact, I was shivering, despite the fact that it was eighty degrees outside.

"Let's get you out of here." He addressed Officer McAfee. "Is she free to go?"

"Yeah. We'll let you guys know if there's anything else we need. Oh, and hey, don't leave town."

There it was—the joking that wasn't. I knew the score. I'd watched Rizzoli & Isles and Criminal Minds. The spouse—or ex-spouse—was always the prime suspect. I suffered no delusions that the Brea Ridge Police Department didn't have me under a microscope.

Ben helped me to my feet and, keeping his arm firmly around my waist, directed me toward the exit.

When I shivered, he moved his hand up to rub my arm. "You're freezing."

"It's the air conditioner in here. I'll be fine once we get into the sunshine." It was the anxiety, and we both knew it. Still, it would be wonderful to get out of that morgue.

He opened the passenger side door of his Jeep, and I climbed inside. He got in, started the car, and the air conditioner was cranked. He quickly turned it off.

"Thanks," I said.

We drove in silence for a minute or two. Then he asked, "How are you feeling?"

"I'm not sure." I squeezed his hand. "Thank you for coming after me. How did you even know I was there?"

"A friend on the force called me."

"Did he tell you anything else about the case? Were there any witnesses? Was anybody seen leaving Todd's hotel room either last night or this morning?"

He didn't answer.

I looked over at his profile and saw a muscle working in his jaw. "Ben, what is it?"

"It's... They don't know much at this point."

"But there's something. And you know what it is. Please tell me."

Ben bit his lower lip. "We'll talk about all this later, Daph. You just identified your ex-husband's body. You don't need to be thinking about his murder right now."

"That's all I can think about," I said. "That and the fact that the police are bound to think I had something to do with it. Sweetheart, please, tell me if you know something I don't."

"Did Officer McAfee mention anything to you about the crime scene?"

"Only that Todd was killed in his hotel room. Why?"

Ben took a deep breath. "It appears that Todd had started writing your name on the wall...in blood...when he died."

* * *

When we got to my house, I was surprised and concerned to see my dad's car in the driveway. I got out of the Jeep as soon as Ben put it in park and hurried inside.

"Dad? Is everything all right?"

"Hey, little girl." He got up from the table where he'd been sitting with Myra and my Uncle Hal and enveloped me in a hug. He smelled like the spicy cologne he'd worn for as long as I could remember.

He and Uncle Hal looked so much alike with their snowy white hair and blue eyes. But Uncle Hal was two years older and quite a bit bigger. He'd always reminded me of a protective bear. When I was a little girl, I'd thought that if I hid behind him, nothing could hurt me. If only things were really that simple.

"What is it?" I asked. "Is it Mom?"

"No, sweetie. We're here for you," he said. "Violet told us what happened yesterday. And Myra filled us in on the rest."

"I'm sorry." Wrapped in my dad's arms, I finally began to cry. "I'm so sorry."

"Shhh. It's all over now."

"No, it's not." I shook my head. "It's not over."

"Come on." He propelled me into the living room. "Why don't we all go in here and relax while we're waiting for Mr. Haynes to get back with that heating element?"

"I'll get Daphne some tea," Myra said.

I drew in a shuddering breath. "I'd prefer water, please."

"Water it is." She brought me a bottle of water from the fridge.

Dad, Ben, and I sat on the sofa. Uncle Hal sat on the pink and white checkered chair, and Myra sat on the ottoman. No one spoke until I'd dried my tears. Myra thoughtfully slipped into the bathroom and brought me a warm washcloth so I could wash my face, and Ben retrieved the lightweight cotton throw from the back of the couch and draped it over my shoulders.

"Hi, Uncle Hal," I said at last.

"Hey, sweetie."

"You look funny sitting in that girly chair."

He grinned. "Don't I though?"

"You want to talk about it?" Dad asked.

"It was him." That's all I could say at the moment. "It was Todd."

"I think it was dreadful the way they dragged you down there and made you look at him," said Myra. "Why couldn't they have brought a photograph or something here to the house?"

"I believe they wanted to gauge my reaction, Myra." At my words, everyone stared at me, except Ben, who looked down at the carpet. "One of the police officers told Ben that before Todd died, he started writing my name on the wall using his blood."

Myra gasped while the men looked grim.

"Why would he do that?" Dad asked.

"I imagine the police believe he was identifying his killer." I rested my head against the back of the sofa.

"But you were with me and Officer McAfee right after Todd was here," Myra said. "Then you were at the police station, then with me and China, and then with Violet and her family all night long. Your alibi is airtight! I'll swear to it."

"Thanks." I smiled slightly. "I appreciate that."

"And I know Violet and Jason will too," she continued. "This is ridiculous. I'm going over to the house and calling Mark. We need some help on this."

Before any of us could react, she was out the front door.

My parents, Uncle Hal, and Aunt Nancy lived two hours away near Roanoke. It dawned on me that it was unusual for them to be here, and I said as much.

"Well, darlin', Vi called your mother last night while you and the little ones were in the kitchen baking cookies or something," Dad said. "She fussed at your mom for giving

Todd your address. Your sister also let her know that she didn't appreciate the fact that he came to see Lucas and Leslie."

"So I guess that's why Mom isn't here?"

"She and your Aunt Nancy will be down later today," Uncle Hal chimed in. "Your dad and I got in the car and came down last night."

"You did what?" My eyes widened. I looked from Uncle Hal to Dad.

"We did," Dad confirmed. "I called Hal as soon as Gloria told me what was going on, and we rode down here to make sure Todd didn't cause any more trouble."

"But where did you stay?"

The two brothers looked at each other and then quickly away.

"Dad?" I urged.

"We didn't stay anywhere."

I looked at Uncle Hal. "What did you do? Drive around all night?"

"For a lot of it, yeah." He shrugged.

My mouth went dry, and I took a drink of the water Myra had brought me. "Did you find him?" My voice emerged as a croak.

"Yeah. Or, at least, we found the truck," said Uncle Hal. "Then we parked in the row behind it at the hotel and slept in the car."

Dad nodded. "We knew that if he came out and got in that truck, one of us would wake up."

"And then what?"

"We were going to call the police and then follow Todd." Dad took my hand. "My family was in danger. You think I was going to go to bed two hours away and let God-knows-what happen to you?"

"Thanks. You too, Uncle Hal."

He merely inclined his head.

"Did you guys happen to notice anyone going into or coming out of Todd's room?" Ben asked.

"No," said Dad. "But that doesn't mean that Todd wasn't dead and his killer already gone by the time we got there."

I was suddenly really glad that Myra had gone to call Mark. I needed all the help I could get.

CHAPTER SEVEN

There was a knock at the side door. I hoped it was Myra and Mark, but it was McElroy Haynes. I was still glad. I desperately needed my oven fixed.

"Are you Daphne?" he asked in a voice as rough as sandpaper.

"I am, Mr. Haynes. I'm sorry I wasn't here to meet you earlier."

"That's all right. Ms. Jenkins was here. You dad and uncle were too." His eyes darted around the room. "They still here?"

"My dad and Uncle Hal are. Myra had to go home."

"Well, I've got your heating element. All I have to do is hook it up and make sure it's working."

"Great," I said. "Thank you. If you don't mind, I'll return to the living room so I won't be in your way. Let me know if you need anything."

"Will do."

Within a few minutes, Mr. Haynes was calling me back into the kitchen.

"I need you to turn the breaker to the oven back on, so I can plug in the element and make sure it's working before I leave."

"All right." I went to the closet where the breaker box was located and flipped the switch.

I came back, and Mr. Haynes had plugged the oven back in and had turned it on. The element began smoking.

"Oh, no!" I rubbed my forehead.

"Good grief, calm down! It's just the coating put on the element by the manufacturer." The grizzled old man glared at me. "That's a sign the thing's working."

"The smoke's not a big deal then," Uncle Hal said from the hallway.

Mr. Haynes' eyes widened. "Not a big deal at all!" He forced a chuckle. "Perfectly natural. Of course, you wouldn't have known that, Daphne. I can see why it might've caused you some concern." He handed me his invoice.

"Let me get my checkbook."

"Well, you can pay me now or you can mail the check. Whatever's best for you is fine with me."

"I'll go ahead and pay you." I passed by Uncle Hal. He was trying hard not to laugh. And Uncle Hal isn't a guy who laughs for no reason. That was curious.

I paid Mr. Haynes, and he left, telling me to be sure and let him know if I had any more trouble with the oven. Before I could get to the bottom of Uncle Hal's amusement, Myra and Mark came in. They, too, used the side door and came on into the kitchen.

"We saw McElroy leaving," Myra said. "Did he get your oven fixed?"

"He did. And I don't know what all the fuss was about him being mean. He was as nice as pie to me." I remembered his overreaction to my concern over the smoke. "There was a second there that I thought he was going to give me a hard time, but he changed his mind."

Myra and Uncle Hal burst out laughing, leaving Mark and me to look on in confusion.

"It seems your Uncle Hal and McElroy Haynes have a history," said Myra.

"It was nothing. And it happened nearly half a century ago." Uncle Hal gave me a sheepish grin. "McElroy had pinched Nancy on the butt while she was at the water fountain. Well, she and I hadn't even started going out yet, but I still took it upon myself to defend her honor."

"You beat him up?"

"I threatened to. To keep from taking a beating, McElroy agreed to back up to that water fountain, turn it on, and get his pants soaked," he said. "That was first thing in the morning, so he had to go most of the day in soggy britches."

"What did he say when people asked why his pants were wet?" I asked.

"He told them to shut up." Uncle Hal shrugged. "Maybe that's when McElroy really started getting an attitude."

"But it seems to go away in your uncle's presence." Myra winked at me. "Glad you can go back to baking, hon."

"Me too. But first, maybe we should see what we can do about this other matter." I turned to Mark. "Thank you so much for coming. Do I need to give you a retainer?"

He shook his head. "Let's see what we've got before we start getting ahead of ourselves."

I asked them if either of them would like something to drink, they declined, and we went into the living room. I brought a chair from the kitchen and sat there so there'd be room for everyone. Ben got up and got himself a chair so he could sit beside me.

Have I mentioned that I love that guy?

Mark Thompson was a broad-shouldered, basically square-shaped man about Myra's age. He had a gray buzz cut, bushy eyebrows, and a gravelly voice. His looks were only semi-deceiving. He could be a rough customer when he had to be.

As a former police officer turned private investigator, I doubted anyone gave him any guff. But he was as nice as could be.

After we'd all gotten seated in the living room and I'd introduced him to Dad and Uncle Hal, Mark took a small notepad and pencil from his shirt pocket.

"While I realize you want to find Todd's killer and, thus, exonerate yourself, Daphne, we need to ensure that there's nothing that could tie you to his murder in any way."

"It's like I said earlier, she was with somebody nearly all of yesterday and last night," Myra said.

"Myra, darlin', I know you're only being helpful, but why don't we let Daphne tell us in her own words?" Mark patted her knee to soften the impact.

"Okay. Well, Myra's right. After I came home and found Todd here, I got away from him as quickly as I could and ran to Myra's house. I burst through her door without even knocking. Sorry about that, by the way."

"No problem, hon. I'd have done the same thing in your situation."

"After you got to Myra's, what happened?" Mark asked.

"She called the police. Officer McAfee responded to the call, and we went through my house to make sure Todd wasn't there and to see whether or not he'd taken anything—"

"And had he?"

"Not that I'm aware of," I said.

"You need to go through your house carefully today— every closet, every drawer, every cabinet—and make sure absolutely nothing is missing." He leveled his gaze at me. "Understand?"

"Y-yes."

"Why?" asked Dad.

"It's important because if Todd took anything from her home, and it's found on his person or at the crime scene, then it could raise the argument that she had been with him."

I hadn't even thought of that. I should've done that yesterday while McAfee was here. But I hadn't known Todd would wind up dead. I wasn't thinking about the possibility of needing to clear myself as a murder suspect. I hadn't really cared if Todd had stolen anything from my home or not, as long as he was gone.

Ben sandwiched my right hand between both of his.

Mark cleared his voice. "After you and Officer McAfee went through the house, what did you do?"

"He went to Myra's house, and I found the note Todd had left on the kitchen table."

"Did you show the note to McAfee?"

I shook my head. "I threw it away. It wasn't threatening, and I saw no reason to give it to him. I did tell him about it though."

"Good. What next?"

I reiterated my steps yesterday and last night. Myra was right. Ninety percent of the time, at least one other person could account for my whereabouts.

"The police will also be looking at your financial records," said Mark.

"Now, hold on!" Uncle Hal protested. "How can they do that?"

"They'll get a warrant. Daphne, have you made any sizeable cash withdrawals lately?"

"Only one that I would consider sizeable—by my standards, anyway—but it was to the wedding planner."

"She asked to be paid in cash?" Mark asked.

"He and yes. He said it would be better for him to have cash so that he could pay the florist and take other expenses out of that money. I don't know what all he's doing." I kinda laughed. "But that's what I'm paying him for, right?"

"What's his name?"

I told him it was Hunter Hampton, and Mark wrote it down.

"Let me get you his card." I went to the bedroom, got the gold foil-embossed business card, and gave it to Mark.

He looked at it and slipped it into his pocket. "I'll check with Mr. Hampton later today. Gentlemen, Myra tells me that you spent the night in the parking lot of the hotel where Mr. Martin was staying?"

Dad and Uncle Hal exchanged glances.

"That's right," Dad said. "We didn't approach his room or anything, so we shouldn't be on any surveillance cameras."

"I might be." Uncle Hal's lips twisted into a grimace. "This darned blood pressure medicine I'm on makes me have to pee all the time."

"Oh, yeah." Dad nodded at Mark. "I'd forgotten about the times one or the other of us had to go inside."

"Did either of you see anyone else go inside?"

"Other people came and went. We didn't pay much attention to them, though, did we, Hal?"

Uncle Hal shook his head. "We were mainly watching for Todd to come out."

"Still, put your heads together once we've finished up here and make a note of every single person you saw going into or coming out of that motel last night," Mark said. "Even if you saw a family leaving, put that down along with a description of every member of that family. Someone might've seen something that could help the police track down the murderer."

I smiled at Mark. I was so glad he was here and taking control of the situation. "What can I do?"

"Dig up all of Todd's old acquaintances. We need to find out if he contacted anyone yesterday—"

"My friend on the police force might be able to help with that," Ben interrupted. "He can at least take a look at Todd's phone and see which numbers he'd called recently."

"Good. Daphne, call his old pals in Tennessee too. And let's find out the exact date he was released. I highly doubt he came straight here from the prison."

"Jason might know that," I said. "He spoke with the warden yesterday to see if Todd was in violation of his parole by being here."

"Was he?" Mark asked.

"He wasn't on parole. He served his full sentence."

"All right. Another call to the warden might be in order to find out who Todd associated with in prison." Mark wrote furiously on the notepad. "You might want to ask Jason to do that since he's already spoken with the warden once and they hopefully already have a good rapport."

"Okay." I was still trying to remember the names of some of Todd's old friends and associates. Even if I remembered who they were, what were the odds of my being able to contact them after all this time?

And what about his parents? Surely, the Brea Ridge Police Department had notified them of his death by now.

"Daphne, are you okay?" Ben's voice sounded as if it was coming from quite a distance away.

"Yeah." I frowned. "Should I call Todd's mother?"

"No," Dad said emphatically. "She and Bert were terrible to you both during and after the trial. Contacting those people will only bring you misery. Let your mother convey our sympathies."

"Yeah, she lives for stuff like that," Uncle Hal added.

Given our assignments, Uncle Hal and Dad set up their conference in the living room, Mark and Myra went to her house, and Ben and I headed into the kitchen.

"I hope you don't mind," I told him, "but I need to get eight cakes made by tomorrow."

"By all means, work. I know it's therapeutic for you."

After I preheated the oven, I got out my favorite blue mixing bowl and four eight-inch, round cake pans. I got my measuring cups and spoons, the recipe, and the necessary ingredients to make the white cakes first.

I'd made them so often, you wouldn't think I'd need a recipe, but I wanted to have it in front of me today. My mind was going in a million different directions.

I measured the flour into the measuring cup and dumped it into the bowl. Next came the sugar.

"I didn't realize we had a wedding planner," Ben said softly.

I looked up, surprised by his comment. "Well...I got overwhelmed. And then, out of the blue, I got a call from this guy who somehow knew the owner of the shop where I bought my wedding gown." I shrugged. "I don't know if I'd looked desperate when I was buying the dress or what, but the guy said he just wanted to offer his services as a wedding planner. He gave me this great spiel about how he'd do it all, and I could merely enjoy the big day."

"Cool. But why didn't you mention it to me? If you had too much wedding stuff on your plate, I'd have been happy to step in and give you a hand."

"I know you would have," I said. "But I didn't want you to think I couldn't do it or that I wasn't enjoying it. I just got so busy. And you were busy too."

He came over and wrapped his arms around my waist. "It's okay. I just want you to know that I don't mind helping. It might be fun."

"All right."

Of course, that was before Myra and Mark returned to tell me that Hunter Hampton, Wedding Planner, was a con man."

CHAPTER EIGHT

"What?!" Not sure people in all the bordering states could hear me, I repeated the word. "What?! He can't be! He…he was in ch-charge of everything!"

Everyone in the house began telling me to calm down. I didn't. I didn't even want to. I wanted to hunt down Hunter Hampton and take my five-thousand-dollar retainer out of his hide.

"What am I going to do?" I paced from the kitchen to the living room and back again.

I didn't know whether to scream, cry, scream and cry, or beg Ben to elope with me. I was back in the living room by now, and I sank onto the sofa before I fainted.

"The flowers, the caterer, the party favors for the reception… We're getting married next Saturday, and none of this is done. Do we even have a church?" I looked at Ben, but he didn't know. How could he?

"I'll take care of it," Myra said.

I hadn't even realized she sat on the sofa beside me. I now turned to look at her. My eyes were full of tears, so she was all blurry. She put her arm around me and pulled me to her. I rested my head on her shoulder and let the tears flow.

"It'll be okay," she said. "We can pull this thing together in two shakes of a lamb's tail."

"Do you really think so?" My voice emerged as a whisper.

"Sure, I do."

"I'll help," Ben volunteered. "Just tell me what needs to be done."

"We're in too," said Dad. "Right, Hal?"

"Uh…yeah. How hard could it be?"

Uncle Hal's response made me sob even harder. How hard could it be? Really hard, since none of us knew what we were doing. But I supposed that even if I wound up carrying a bouquet of dandelions and serving sweet tea and cheeseburgers at the reception, Ben and I would still be just as married.

Still, I hated that I'd gotten us into this mess. Why had I ever trusted Hunter Hampton? Because he was a charming, slick salesman—or, rather, con man—who'd made me believe that I could put my wedding in his hands and not have to worry about anything but walking down the aisle.

Either I hadn't heard the doorbell or Dad had merely opened the door when he saw the women approaching, but when I looked up, there stood Mom and Aunt Nancy.

"Daphne, what're you going on about?" Mom asked. "If you're truly this upset that Todd is dead, you should've never gotten that restraining order. You should've sat down with the man and heard him out."

If it hadn't been for Dad, I think I might've told Mom right then and there to turn around and go back home. Instead, I merely glared at her and lowered my eyes again.

Myra—my surrogate mom—jumped to my defense. "She's not upset about him." The word dripped with contempt. "She's crying because she was duped by a thieving, no-good, conniving, back-stabbing con man who convinced her he was a wedding planner."

"Oh, my," said Aunt Nancy, a tall, elegant brunette who favored year-round pantsuits. Today's suit was a short-sleeved, turquoise number. On her, it looked good. "But the wedding is in a matter of days! Is there anything we can do to help?"

"We'll just have to plan the thing ourselves," Mom said. She was quite a bit shorter than Aunt Nancy and kept her hair dyed blonde. She and Violet looked a lot alike. But whereas Vi came off as cute and pixie-like, Mom's typical facial expression was one of foreboding and harsh judgment.

As you might have surmised by this point, Mom and I were constantly butting heads. She'd had a heart attack last year, and we'd both been trying harder since her health scare. But we couldn't help but argue. We were just too different.

"Myra has already volunteered for the job," I said.

"Oh." Mom tightened her lips and raised her chin.

"The two of you are welcome to help out if you'd like," Myra said. "The gentlemen have already offered their services."

Mom raised and lowered one shoulder. "We'll see. But I'm sure you have it covered."

I was relieved when the timer went off on the oven and I had a reason to leave the room. I excused myself and went into the kitchen.

Using the oven mitts, I removed the two white cakes from the oven and sat the pans on a baking rack. I had more white cake batter ready to go into two additional eight-inch, round pans, so I poured the batter into the pans, put the pans into the oven, and reset the timer.

Ben came into the kitchen and put his arms around me. I slumped against him.

"I'm so sorry," I said.

"It's all right."

"It's not all right." I could hear the buzz of conversation coming from the living room, but I lowered my voice anyway. "Not only did I manage to lose us five-thousand dollars, none of the arrangements are made for our wedding."

He kissed my forehead. "Come next Saturday, we'll be married. And with Myra and all the people in Brea Ridge who care about you—and my mom, I know she'll love to help— it'll be a beautiful ceremony and reception."

"Do you promise?"

"I promise," he said.

"Even if the ceremony takes place at the jail?" After all, I was still under scrutiny by the police with regard to Todd's death.

"You aren't going to be in jail. People who love you are working on that too."

"I'll have to take your word for it." I tightened my grip around his waist. "I love you."

"I love you."

"Never let go, okay?"

"I won't," he said.

* * *

By the time the other two white cakes had finished baking, I was desperate to get out of the house. I hid my unsweetened cocoa behind a bag of flour and asked Ben if he would take me to Save-A-Buck to get some cocoa.

"Of course." He looked around the living room. "Anyone else need anything?"

Only Dad, Mom, Uncle Hal, and Aunt Nancy remained. Myra and Mark had vamoosed shortly after Mom and Aunt Nancy had arrived.

"I wouldn't mind a case of beer," Uncle Hal said.

"Now, Hal, you don't need any beer." Aunt Nancy looked mortified at the thought that her husband had made any request at all, much less for beer.

"We'll get it," I said, with a wink at Aunt Nancy.

As soon as Ben and I got into his Jeep, I asked him to take me to Jason and Violet's house. "I'd like to talk with them before Lucas and Leslie get home from day camp."

"No problem." He grinned. "By the way, I saw you hide that can of cocoa."

I gasped. "Do you think anyone else saw?"

He laughed. "No. I don't think so."

"I just had to get out of there. Mom's long-suffering expression and her accusatory tone was driving me up the wall." I groaned. "Please tell me I'm adopted."

"You're adopted."

"I guess it would mean more if I really thought it was true. Maybe I could pretend I'm Dad's love child with Elizabeth Taylor." I tried to think of another actress who could be my mother, but I couldn't come up with anyone better than Liz.

When we got to my sister's house, I was relieved to find that I was right about the kids not being home yet. Unfortunately, Jason wasn't home yet either.

"You've been crying." Violet took me by the shoulders. "What is it? What happened?"

So I started at the beginning and gave her the play-by-play of the entire day. "And it's only two-thirty. Could I crawl under your bed and hide until tomorrow?"

"I wish you could," she said. "But Dad and Uncle Hal would form a search party."

"And your Mom would think we'd eloped," Ben said.

"Let's do that! Then later on we can have a reception." I smiled. "Sounds like a plan to me."

"Daphne, you look serious." Violet's eyes searched mine. "You know how hurt Lucas and Leslie would be if you didn't include them in your wedding."

"Oh. Right. And Ben's parents. And Dad."

"And me!" she said.

"I know. I was only talking."

"You were not only talking. All it would've taken is for Ben to say come on, and you'd have been in the Jeep on your way to Vegas or somewhere."

"Vi, it's just been an impossible day, okay?"

Her voice softened. "I know. So before the kids get here, tell me what I can do to help."

"Would you ask Jason to call the warden again and try to find out the names of the people who might've associated with Todd while he was in prison?" I asked. "Mark thinks that since Jason has already spoken with the warden once, they'll have already established a rapport."

"Okay. I can do that. And Jason is already planning Ben's bachelor party, so that's taken care of."

"At this point, it's about the only thing."

She frowned. "If I could get my hands on that guy…"

"You and me both," said Ben.

"Ben and I are going over to China's house when we leave here," I said. "If anybody will know where we can find Hunter Hampton—or whoever he is—China will."

* * *

China lived in a modest gable-front home on the outskirts of Brea Ridge. When Ben and I arrived, she was sitting on her front porch. She had a navy blue, metal glider and two rockers—one on either side of the glider—and she sat on the rocker nearest the front door.

"Welcome!" She had to shout over the five or six dogs in the fenced backyard that had started barking when we'd driven up. "Hush up back there!"

The dogs paid no attention to her scolding.

"They'll be quiet in a minute." She got up and gave me a hug. "What a day you've had."

"Are you talking about Todd or the wedding planner?" I asked, as I took a seat on the glider. Ben sat down beside me.

"Well, hon, I was talking about the ex-husband. Isn't that enough?" China asked.

"You'd think so, but then I had to find out that the wedding planner I'd hired is a con man. He took my money and left me high and dry."

She frowned. "Have you called him?"

"Yes, but the call went to voicemail."

"What did you say to him?"

"I didn't say anything. I didn't know what to say."

"Just hung up then?" she asked.

I nodded.

"Good. If he calls back, play along like you don't know anything is wrong. Ask if he needs anything."

"Oh, that's a good idea!" Ben leaned forward with his elbows on his knees. "He'll still think she's none the wiser and might agree to meet thinking Daphne is going to give him more money."

China smiled. "And that's when we'll nab him."

"You know, you really missed your calling," I said.

"Nah. I have lots of callings. I heed them all." She slowly rocked as she studied the horizon. "So you don't think any of your wedding has been planned, huh?"

"Only the bachelor party. Jason is taking care of that."

"Well, that's not exactly the wedding, unless you're planning on jumping out of the cake and marrying Ben on the spot."

"That'd work for me," Ben said.

"I asked him to elope with me when we were at Violet's house earlier," I explained to China. "She didn't take that very well."

"No, I don't imagine she would. She and her family love you and want to be part of your special day. We all do." She turned to me with a bright smile. "It'll work out. Always does."

"Myra volunteered to take over."

"Jesus, help us all." China's shoulders shook with laughter. "I'm just kidding, of course. Myra will…well, she'll get the job done."

"Yeah, I know."

"So what's being done about investigating Todd's murder?" she asked. "Is Mark on that?"

"Yes, and he's given us all assignments."

"I'll call him later to see how I can help. And I'll see what I can do to help Myra too." Her eyes sparkled with amusement. "I told you I have many callings."

* * *

At the Save-A-Buck, Ben and I decided to divide and conquer. We couldn't simply buy cocoa and go home given the length of time we'd been gone. So, we bought cocoa, steaks, potatoes, macaroni, eggs, rolls, tomatoes, and bagged salad.

When we got back to the house, though, Dad, Mom, Uncle Hal, and Aunt Nancy weren't there. Mom had left a note on the kitchen table.

Violet invited us to dinner, so we're eating with them. We'll see you tomorrow.

I turned to Ben and released a breath I hadn't even realized I'd been holding.

"Thank goodness! Remind me to tell Vi how much I love her!"

CHAPTER NINE

Not wanting all that food to go to waste—and, besides, we were hungry—Ben put the steaks on the grill and washed the potatoes. Meanwhile, I transferred the white cakes to cardboard rounds and mixed up the batter for the chocolate cakes. By the time Ben had finished preparing our meal of steaks, baked fries, and salad, two of the cakes were in the oven.

"You looked more relaxed than I've seen you all day," Ben said, as I filled his glass with sweet tea.

"Well, there are two reasons for that. One, I'm confident that I'll be able to deliver the baked goods to Save-A-Buck first thing tomorrow morning. So that's great." I sat back down across from Ben. "I can't control much after Hurricane What-the-Crap blew through here and turned my life upside down, but that I can control."

"And two?"

"My mother is at Violet's house."

He raised his glass. "There is that."

I clinked my glass to his. "I don't know why that woman drives me so insane, but she does. For instance, did I tell you that she's the one who gave Todd my address? Why in the world would she do that?"

"I have no idea, babe." He took a drink of tea before putting his glass back down. "Maybe she thought you needed some closure."

"I got closure the day I walked out of Todd's sentencing hearing."

Ben looked down at his plate. "It's all right if you need to talk about it."

"About what?"

"Todd. The good, the bad…how you felt today when you identified his body."

I swallowed the lump that had formed in my throat. "Today was hard. I felt sorry for him…sad that so much of his life had been unfulfilled. Even before he was killed, he was in prison. And before that, he wasn't happy." I took a sip of my tea. "The only time I saw him truly content with his life was when he was in college."

"That is sad."

I nodded. "Nothing ever equaled that high to Todd of being the big man on campus."

The phone rang just as the oven timer went off.

"That might be Mark," I said. "Would you mind answering the phone while I grab the cakes?"

"No problem."

While Ben spoke with the person on the phone, I got the first two cakes out of the oven and put the other two in. I set the timer and returned to the table where I determined from hearing his end of the conversation that the person Ben was talking with was either Jason or Violet.

He handed me the receiver. "Violet wants to speak with you."

"Hey, Vi."

"She's coming," Jason said. "I just wanted to see how you're doing."

"I'm all right. Thanks."

"We're here if you need us, you know."

"I do know," I said. "Did you speak with the warden?"

"Yeah. Ben will tell you all about it. Here's Violet."

My sister skipped the pleasantries. "I got Mom alone and asked her if she'd lost her mind."

My jaw dropped. Violet was the golden child. She and Mom were as close as a mother and daughter could be. I couldn't imagine her confronting our mother like that.

"She pretended she didn't know what I was talking about," Vi continued. "But I didn't back down. I said I could hardly believe she'd not only told Todd where to find you but that she'd apparently encouraged him to see Leslie and Lucas."

Ah, there it was. Violet's protection and love for her children outweighed any affection she had for another person, even Mom.

"Let me guess—she denied ever encouraging him to see the children," I said.

"No! She didn't! She said she thought it would be good for him to see them, how much they've grown, and how beautiful they are."

"And what did she think it would be like for them to see him?" I huffed. "I guess they could see if they could remember their uncle at all since they've hardly ever seen him in their entire lives."

"Exactly." She gave a growl of frustration. "Mom knows better than that."

"So what reason did she give for spilling my address?"

Violet didn't answer right away, and I had to prompt her to do so.

"She thought he deserved to see you," she said at last. "He was your husband—blah, blah, blah. You really don't want to hear her warped reasoning."

I debated the issue in my mind. "No. I guess I don't."

After all, Mom had thought I'd pushed Todd into shooting at me in the first place. *You know how you can be, Daphne.* And she'd dubbed me cruel for divorcing him while he was in prison.

"What I can't figure out is why he even wanted to come here," I said. "All those years he was in prison, I never heard a word from him—good or bad. Then he gets out of prison and just shows up here in Brea Ridge? There's bound to be a reason."

"I agree. And whatever that reason is, I bet it's ultimately what got him killed."

* * *

Ben sat on a stool at the island while I placed the first of the eight cakes on a turntable. I put a cake icer tip in my piping bag and then filled the bag with white buttercream.

"So what did Jason tell you about his conversation with the warden?" I asked, as I gently squeezed the piping bag and slowly spun the turntable to frost the sides of the cake.

"He said Todd didn't appear to have many friends in prison, but the one person he was known to associate with— Monty Harlow—got out two weeks before Todd was released."

I iced the top of the cake and then used a spatula to smooth it out. "When was that?"

"Just over a month ago."

"That makes this whole thing ever weirder, don't you think?" I scraped the excess icing back into the bowl. "I knew his coming here had nothing—or else very little—to do with me. What was he after?"

"We need to find this Monty Harlow and see what he knows."

* * *

The next morning, I put all of the baked goods into the back of the Mini Cooper and set off for Save-A-Buck. Luckily, Steve had been watching for me, and he and a couple of bag boys came out to help me carry everything inside.

There were two tables near the front of the store that had been pushed together and covered with white linen tablecloths. A banner hung from one end of the tables to the other and read, "Baked goods provided by Daphne's Delectable Cakes."

"Ms. Jenkins was in late yesterday afternoon." Steve put the boxes he was carrying down on one of the tables. "She told me what a rough time you've been having."

"Yes, well..." I wasn't sure if he was talking about the oven, Todd, or the business about the wedding planner. With Myra, I never knew.

"I'm really sorry. To think you had everything taken care of, and then to learn that your wedding planner has taken off with your money..." He sighed. "That's terrible."

"Well, he still might call." I knew better, but I was trying to be optimistic there in the store in front of Steve Franklin and the Save-A-Buck employees.

Juanita, my favorite cashier, came over and hugged me. "I am so sorry for your misfortune. I have taken classes in floral arrangement, so please let me help with your flowers."

"All right," I said. "I will. That is, if the guy doesn't call me back and tell me I'm overreacting."

"Okay."

"And I'll get with my distributors to have the flowers and food obtained at a wholesale price for you," said Steve.

"Thank you. I'm truly grateful."

When I left the Save-A-Buck, I drove straight to Myra's house. She apparently hadn't been out of bed for long and was still wearing her robe and fuzzy slippers.

"Goodness," she said as she opened the door. "What's happened now?"

"Well, I just came from the Save-A-Buck. Steve Franklin is offering me a discount on food and flowers, and Juanita has volunteered to do my floral arrangements."

"That's wonderful!" She frowned. "Isn't it?"

"Yes, except that I thought we were keeping the news about the wedding planner under wraps until we saw whether or not he'd call me back."

"Has he called you back?"

"No."

"Well, there you go." She motioned me into the kitchen. "Coffee?"

"Yes, please." I noticed as I sat down at the kitchen table that Bruno was playing outside in the yard.

I mulled over what Myra and Mark had told me about the wedding planner. He'd told the proprietor of the dress shop that he was new in the wedding planning business but that he'd overseen the weddings of several of his friends. He'd provided photos of beautiful, elaborate weddings. Those were the same photos he'd shown me.

The proprietor had given the wedding planner the contact information for several women who had upcoming weddings. When Mark followed up with these women, he learned that they had not been contacted by Hunter Hampton. I was the only one.

Myra sat a cup of coffee in front of me. She knew I liked my coffee with cream and sugar, so it was perfect.

"Why do you think he targeted me?" I asked.

"I'm not so sure it was you in particular, hon. I think that the first person who took the bait, he'd take her money and run."

"But why? Why not get all the money he could before skipping out?" I sipped the hot coffee. "It doesn't make any sense to stop with one person."

"No, I guess it doesn't. But don't you let that worry you. I'm going to take care of all the wedding preparations," she said. "Thank you for telling me about Steve and Juanita. I'll add them to the list."

"There's already a list?"

She smiled. "Of course."

"Jason called last night and told Ben that a man named Marty Harlow—either a friend or associate of Todd's—was released just two weeks prior to Todd's release. And—get this—Todd has been out of prison for over a month."

"Well, he took his sweet time getting here to confess his undying devotion, didn't he?"

I nodded. "I knew all along that's not why he was here. But why was he? And why was he trying to write my name on the wall when he died?"

"We'll get all that figured out. Leave it to Mark." She got up to get a pen and a notepad out of a kitchen drawer. When she sat back down, she wrote Marty Harlow on the pad. "I'll have Mark see what he can dig up on this guy."

"Thanks, Myra."

"It'll be all right." She reached over and squeezed my hand.

"I talked to Violet last night. And, are you ready for this?" Myra leaned closer. "Yes."

"She really let Mom have it."

"Good for her! What did she say?"

"She asked why in the world Mom would give Todd my address and then encourage him to see the twins."

"Wait," she said. "Your mom actually suggested that Todd go see Lucas and Leslie? Is she out of her mind?"

"Actually, I believe that she always thought Todd wasn't that bad." I huffed. "She'd have known better had she lived with the man. But, anyway, she thought it would be good for Todd to see the kids and that seeing me would give us both closure."

"The man almost gave you closure from your entire life once. Wasn't that enough?"

"Apparently not," I said.

Myra slowly shook her head. "I just can't comprehend that—taking the feelings of somebody else, especially a jerk like Todd Martin, into consideration over those of your own children."

"I know." I blew out a breath. "But, then, that's Mom. She always liked Todd."

"I have never liked Todd. Never!"

I started laughing. "Myra, you never knew the man!"

"I didn't have to. I know you. That's enough."

CHAPTER TEN

I decided to go with chocolate pound cake for the base tier of the wedding cake. Lucas and Leslie loved chocolate. By alternating layers with vanilla pound cake, everyone should be happy. When I preheated the oven to three-hundred-fifty degrees, I was delighted all over again to have a working oven.

It took an especially large batch of batter for the fourteen-inch cake. I whisked the flour and salt together in a large bowl and set the mixture aside. Then I put the butter and sugar into the bowl of my stand mixer and beat them at medium speed.

I didn't realize Myra and Mark had come in through the kitchen door until she called my name. I started and then turned off the mixer.

"You scared me."

"Why didn't you have the door locked?" Myra asked. "We could've been anybody!"

"Not Todd. And he's the reason I was locking the doors."

"But someone killed Todd," Mark reminded me. "You really need to keep your doors locked."

"Yeah, I guess I do." I turned and added the vanilla and cocoa to the mixing bowl. "Give me just one second, will you?"

I finished the batter and poured it into the prepared pan. I slid the pan into the oven and set the timer.

"There we go. We've got plenty of time to talk now." I gestured toward the coffee pot. "Would either of you like a cup of coffee?"

"Sure," Mark said.

I put sugar, artificial sweetener, and creamer on the table and poured us all a cup of coffee. I placed their cups in front of them, and before I could get mine, I noticed that Mark had a photo of Hunter Hampton on the table next to him.

"Why do you have a photo of Hunter?" I asked. "Did you find him?"

Mark frowned and then exchanged glances with Myra. "You think this is Hunter Hampton?"

"It is," I said. "Who did you think it was?"

"This is Monty Harlow, Todd's old prison buddy."

I slid my chair out and dropped onto it. "You've got to be kidding me."

"No, hon, he's not." Myra got up and got my coffee. "Here. You probably need this."

"I need something a lot stronger than this. Something that could turn back time would be nice." I stared at the photo of Hunter or Monty or whoever he was. "So he was only here to play me."

"We figured that already," Myra pointed out. "You know, since he didn't contact any of the other women from the bridal store."

"But now we know why," I said. "He did it for Todd."

"We don't really know why." Mark added sugar to his coffee. "Yes, he was likely here at Todd's behest. But why? Was Todd desperate for money? Was he trying to ruin your wedding? We need to find out exactly what they were after."

"And how do we do that if we can't get Hun—Monty—to call me back?"

"What types of voicemail messages have you left him?" Mark asked.

"None. I've been so angry that I've simply hung up without saying anything."

"Good. We can work with that." Mark took out a notebook. "I want you to call him, and I'm going to tell you exactly what to say."

"That won't work," I protested. "He won't call me back. Besides, everybody in Brea Ridge knows by now that my wedding planner was a phony."

Mark kept writing. "Doesn't matter. You can leave a message, and he isn't local. So he has no idea what the people in town know or don't know."

"Right." Myra gave a resolute nod. "He's not in our clique. Doesn't know the secret handshake and isn't privy to the gossip."

"Okay. But, if Monty was working with Todd, then he's bound to know that he was found dead yesterday morning."

"Not necessarily," he said. "And, even if he does, he won't know for sure whether or not the gig is up until he hears from you. So call him, and leave him this message."

I read Mark's note and then got up to get my phone.

Myra was reading the message when I got back. "Yeah, this'll work. If he thinks there's still a chance he can bilk you for a little more money, he will."

I called. As anticipated, the call went directly to voicemail.

"Hi, Hunter. This is Daphne Martin. I haven't talked with you in a day or two. Things have been really crazy around here—you wouldn't believe. Anyway, the wedding date is drawing ever closer, and I'm getting more nervous by the minute. Do you have everything taken care of? Is there anything else we need to do—anyone who needs to be paid? Please give me a call back. Thanks."

I ended the call and looked at Mark. "Now what?"

"We wait. Or rather, you wait. If you hear from Harlow, you act like everything is fine—except that you're really nervous about the wedding and everything coming together. Give him a chance to talk. If he calls, it's going to be because he thinks he can get more money from you."

"Should she invite the bum over here so we can nab him?" Myra asked.

"Where did you meet before, Daphne?"

"We met outside the Save-A-Buck."

"Well, you can't do that now." Myra turned to Mark. "She can't meet him at the Save-a-Buck. Somebody might come up and say something about the wedding."

"That's right," Mark said. "Have him come here but only when you know that I can be here. And I'd like to have McAfee—or some other cop—here too. Not only will it help with your defense, but they can arrest the guy and find out what he's up to. Odds are, he's the one who killed Todd."

I shivered from the chill that tingled through my body. "I hadn't considered that."

"That's why we want you to keep your doors locked!" Myra rolled her eyes and then sipped her coffee. "Maybe Todd was trying to write you a note to warn you when he died."

Before I could respond, my phone rang. I didn't recognize the number. I answered and put the phone on speaker.

"Daphne, sweetie, how are you?" asked the man I'd known as Hunter Hampton.

"I'm getting antsy, Hunter. How's everything going?"

"Well, the florist is hounding me to get a little more of the money up front. Is that doable?"

"Yeah, sure. How much do you need?"

"A thousand should do it."

"Okay," I said. "I'll write you a check. Hey, do you mind coming here? I've got a cake in the oven, and I can't leave."

Mark gave me the "okay" sign.

"No problem. What's your address?"

I rattled off the address, and Hunter/Monty said he'd be at my house within the hour. I ended the call and looked at my co-conspirators.

"And now we wait?"

Mark shook his head. "Now we get prepared. I'll call McAfee and tell him to park on the next block over so Harlow won't be spooked when he arrives."

"I can go pick up Officer McAfee if he'd like for me to," Myra said.

"I don't think that'll be necessary. He's fit enough to walk a block." Mark arched a brow. "I have to keep both eyes on you all the time, don't I?"

She winked. "No need to be jealous. My heart belongs to you."

* * *

An hour and a half later, Mark, Myra, Officer McAfee, and I were crouching on my living room floor with the curtains drawn.

"Call him one more time," said McAfee. "If he doesn't answer, we give up. He's not coming."

I nodded and made the call. It went directly to voicemail. "Hi, Hunter. It's Daphne. Do you need to reschedule? Let me know what's going on. Thanks."

McAfee stood. "We'll give him fifteen minutes. If he hasn't called or shown up by then, I've got to go. You stay inside with your doors locked and don't answer the door if he comes by here, Ms. Martin. Got it?"

"Got it."

Apparently pretty certain that Harlow wasn't going to arrive, McAfee went into the kitchen. "Dang, this cake looks good."

"Come to the wedding, and you can have a piece," I said.

"Might just do that." He smiled. "I'm sorry this guy jerked you around." The smile faded as he encompassed Mark and Myra in his gaze. "And even though it seems like he could've been working with your ex-husband, that's purely conjecture at this time. We need to interrogate him to learn the truth about what he's doing, who he is or was working for, and where he was at the time of Todd Martin's murder."

Fifteen minutes crawled by, mainly with Mark and me hemming and hawing and trying to make polite conversation to pass the time while Myra looked at Officer McAfee as if he'd just stepped down from Mount Olympus.

"Folks, please do as I've asked you to do, and leave the investigation to me and the rest of the Brea Ridge Police Department." With that, McAfee headed for the front door.

"Wait!" I called. "What about Monty Harlow? What will you do about him?"

"I'll have my men looking for him."

Officer McAfee left, and I turned to Mark with a sigh. "Great. Harlow will probably show up as soon as McAfee gets out of sight."

"If he does, Myra and I'll still be here."

"You don't think he's coming either, do you?"

He shook his head.

"But why?" I walked to the side door and looked out the window to make sure there weren't any cars headed in our direction. "Do you think he was on to us?"

"I honestly don't know," Mark said. "Either something spooked him, or he decided to get out while he still could. Maybe he hadn't known about Todd's body being found and then saw it in today's paper or something."

Myra peered over my shoulder. "Or maybe lightning struck him when he went out to get in his car."

"There's not a cloud in the sky, sugar plum."

I had to agree with Mark. We couldn't have asked for a more beautiful day.

"So? That doesn't stop the Lord from striking down the wicked if He takes a notion," she said. "And a man who'd steal a woman's wedding money is wicked."

"Have you personally ever known any wicked person— say, in the past century—to get struck by lightning?" Mark asked.

I closed my eyes, knowing it was coming.

"Oh, honey."

There it was.

"Why don't we go back into the living room and get comfortable?" I asked. Mark simply nodded and led the way.

Myra didn't need to be prodded to continue her story.

"One beautiful day—not a cloud in the sky, mind you— Leroy Millsap decided he'd call on the Widow Spencer. Now Widow Spencer was a nice looking woman, and her husband had died at a fairly young age working in the coal mines, so Widow Spencer wasn't too awfully old herself."

"How old are we talking?" Mark asked.

"I'd say mid-forties or thereabouts. Anyhow, Widow Spencer was outside hanging a load of clothes on the line. Now she lived out in Ford's Holler and didn't have a single neighbor for miles. And Leroy Millsap never did have an ounce of propriety about him anyway, so he just whipped it on out."

"Whipped it on out?" I echoed.

"Yep. He whipped it out and lightning struck him right on it." She gave an emphatic nod. "The paramedic said that if Leroy hadn't been wearing his tennis shoes, it'd have killed him."

Mark looked confused. "What about her?"

"Oh, I don't know if she was wearing tennis shoes or not."

"I mean, didn't the lightning hurt her?"

"Oh, no, honey. It seems Leroy was packing a thumbtack instead of a rail spike, so she wasn't anywhere near the thing when he got struck. Or should I say smote?"

Mark opened his mouth, closed it again, and looked down at the rug between his feet.

"So you see, sometimes the Lord'll just smite evildoers if He takes a notion," Myra said. "He did that day, and he might've today too."

Like Mark, I had nothing to say. In fact, we sat in awkward silence until my phone rang.

It was Officer McAfee. "Ms. Martin, I called to let you know for certain that your wedding planner—or fake wedding planner—won't be arriving at your house today. So, you don't have to be concerned about that any longer."

"Did you find him?"

"Yes, ma'am. He's—"

"Did he confess?" I interrupted, eager to get the whole Todd-Hunter-Monty fiasco behind me. "Did he tell you why he duped me?"

"No, Ms. Martin. He's dead. Shot in the chest—just like your ex-husband."

CHAPTER ELEVEN

"What is it?" Myra asked as soon as I put down my phone.

"It's the wedding planner. He was found shot to death. Just like Todd." I slumped in the chair. "How can this be happening?"

"That's what we need to figure out." Mark stood. "I'll go back the newspaper office and get Ben. I'll fill him in on the way to the police station, and we'll see what we can find out there. Meanwhile, you two stay together—preferably here—and keep the doors locked."

"We aren't going anywhere," Myra said. "Just get back here as soon as you know something."

He gave her a peck on the lips. "I will. You two be careful."

"You be careful."

As soon as Mark left, I decided to call China. "I need to let her know what's going on. I asked her to see what she could find out about the wedding planner—of course, this was before I knew he was in cahoots with Todd—and I might've been putting her in danger."

She didn't answer her phone.

"I really might've put her in danger, Myra." I stood and began to pace. "This is terrible. If anything has happened to her, I'll never forgive myself."

"China is tougher than anybody I know. St. Peter will probably have to knock her in the head on Judgment Day."

About that time, a vehicle roared up into my driveway. My eyes widened as I stared at Myra. She simply shook her head. "That's her. I'd recognize the sound of China York's little pickup truck anywhere."

She was right. I looked out the window, and here came China with her shotgun in her arms. I quickly went to the kitchen and unlocked the door to let her in.

"Heard what happened over the scanner." She propped the gun against the wall by the door. "McAfee answered the call. Said he was en route from your street, so I figured the murder victim had something to do with Todd Martin."

"It was the wedding planner," Myra said. "Mark has gone to get Ben, and they're going to the police station to see what they can find out."

"Come on in and have a seat." I led the way to the living room. "Anybody want anything to drink?"

They both said they were fine, so we all sat down.

"We need to get to the bottom of this." China took a small spiral notebook from the pocket of her red plaid shirt. "Daphne, got a pen?"

I went back to the kitchen and got China a pen.

China flipped open the notebook. "First, let's go over what we know. Todd came to town two days ago."

"As far as we know." Myra spread her hands. "He could've been here for days but didn't show up to Daphne's house until then."

"Good point. Daphne, when did this wedding planner guy first get in touch with you?"

"Well over a month ago."

"And you said that Jason found out that Todd had been out for two months, right?" Myra asked.

I nodded. "So the two of them had planned this all along. But why? That's the part I can't figure out."

Myra leaned forward and put on her therapy-is-now-in-session face. "The man told you he loved you. Now, we know that if he did, he certainly had an odd way of showing it, but is it possible that is why he came here to Brea Ridge?"

"I don't think so," I said. "He was in prison for seven years. In all that time, I didn't get one phone call, one card, one letter, one email saying as much as hello. Then he shows up here and says he's had all this time to think and that he's still in love with me? I don't buy it."

"I'm not buying it either." China tapped the pen on the notebook. "He wanted something. Judging by his connection with this wedding planner fellow, I'm guessing Todd needed money. He couldn't come right out and ask you, given the fact that you were divorced and he'd just finished a stint in prison for trying to kill you."

"So he talked with my mom, found out what was going on in my life, and cooked up this wedding planner scheme." I leaned my head back against the chair and looked up at the ceiling. "I knew I shouldn't have trusted that Hunter or Monty or whatever you want to call him. But he had these great references, and I thought he could really be a help to me."

"Of course, you did. Although why you didn't run the idea by me or Ben or someone first is beyond me." Myra was obviously miffed because I hadn't asked her to plan my wedding in the first place.

"I thought I could handle it all myself," I said. "It didn't seem like such a big deal at first. And then cake orders picked up, and I got slammed."

"I know." Myra sighed. "I just wish you'd come to me, that's all."

"I wish I had too. But I didn't want to impose."

China scoffed. "We're family. Helping each other is never an imposition. Now, back to business. If Todd was getting his money though the wedding planner scheme, then why did he show up here?"

"You're right." I inclined my head. "He could've stayed in the background, and I'd have kept giving the wedding planner money until the day of the wedding when I learned that nothing had been done." I blew out a breath. "Thank goodness I found out in time. I'd have been devastated."

"Something made him desperate," said Myra. "He either needed more money faster than it was coming in, or else he wanted you to do something for him and believed he could manipulate you into doing it."

I gave this some thought. "Before Todd went to prison, he had a good job in a local manufacturing plant. In fact, he was a shift supervisor. But he'd have been hard pressed to find work after serving time for assault with a deadly weapon."

"Okay." Myra rubbed the underside of her chin. "So Todd runs through whatever money he had, and what does he do now? He can't find a job. He's trying to walk the straight and narrow, but now he can't." She flung her arms out, nearly hitting China. "He wants out, but they keep pulling him back in! Like in that movie, right? So he calls his old pal Monty. 'Monty, buddy, I'm in a bind. Help a fellow out here.' And so they cook up this scheme to get money and get back at the old ball and chain at the same time."

"I can see that," said China. "But let's also consider this. Monty Harlow might not have been the only friend Todd turned to."

I groaned. "I need to be baking. Could we please move this conversation to the kitchen?"

"Sure, hon." Myra was the first to stand. "Did you get a new order in?"

"I'm supposed to have a carved dog done by Sunday, but I'd like to get another tier of the wedding cake baked. That doesn't require a lot of concentration at this point, but it gives me something to do so I don't go crazy."

I preheated the oven and got the clean mixing bowl out of the dishwasher.

China ambled into the kitchen and leaned against the island. "What did you do in Tennessee? Your job, I mean."

"I was an administrative assistant for a government housing agency," I said. "Why?"

"Well, I'm just trying to figure how you tie in to all this—except for the fact that you were married to Todd Martin. It's either like Myra said and you were the one person he believed he could manipulate into helping him, or there was more to his choosing you than meets the eye."

"I don't know why or how my old job could factor into Todd's choice of a patsy." I put butter and shortening into the bowl and turned the mixer on low. "I haven't worked there in over a year, and I'm only close to one person who's still with the agency. Besides, how could government housing factor into some sort of criminal enterprise?"

"And Todd and the wedding planner are both dead." Myra joined us at the island. "So no matter what they were up to, their boss or some other third party wound up killing them both, right?"

"Looks that way," said China.

"Then why would the third guy kill Todd and Harlow unless he didn't need them anymore? And if Daphne here was the target in their schemes all along, why would guy number three kill the wedding planner and Todd—especially Todd—if he wanted to get close to Daphne?"

"I did get the emergency order of protection," I said. "Maybe that clued the third guy in to the fact that I didn't want anything to do with Todd."

Myra shook her head. "I don't think so. We don't think Todd knew about the EPO because he didn't try to make contact with you later that night. I think he was going to try again the next day. And if Todd didn't know about the EPO, then guy number three wouldn't know about it either. Unless he was having you tailed or something."

I slowly added sugar to the butter and shortening mixture. "As paranoid as I've been after finding Todd in my kitchen, I believe I'd have noticed if someone was following me."

"True." China squinted at a spot just above my head. Had I not known that she tended to do this when she was deep in thought, then I'd have looked to see if there was a spider on the wall behind me. "What I can't figure out is why our third guy would kill the other two."

"He didn't need them anymore," said Myra. "That's the only thing it could be."

* * *

Ben and Mark came in about twenty minutes after I'd put the cake in the oven.

Stopping in the kitchen to breathe deeply, Ben smiled. "Heaven."

"It does smell good in here, doesn't it?" Mark sniffed the air. "Yesterday it was chocolate, and today it's vanilla."

I explained how I was alternating flavors of the wedding cake tiers with chocolate and vanilla pound cake.

"How many pieces of each can I have without looking like a pig?" Mark asked.

"As many as you want." I patted his shoulder and then turned to give Ben a kiss before we went into the living room. "What's the word at the station?"

Mark sat on the sofa beside Myra. "Monty Harlow and Hunter Hampton were definitely the same person. The vic had a bunch of the wedding planner business cards on him when he was found."

"He had some other interesting cards in his wallet too," said Ben, sitting on the pink-and-white gingham chair. "In addition to your Daphne's Delectable Cakes business card, he had one from Chilton Housing Authority. Isn't that where you worked in Tennessee?"

I sat on the arm of Ben's chair and put my arm around his shoulders. "It is."

"Told you," said China. "I told Myra and Daphne that Todd's coming here and whatever shady dealing got him killed might've had something to do with where she used to work."

"But that doesn't make sense," Ben said. "Daphne hasn't worked there in well over a year."

"Are you still friends with some of the employees?" Mark asked.

"Only one. Her name is Bonnie, and she works in the accounting department. But I doubt Todd would have known that I still keep in touch with her. Even when things were going normally in our marriage—for us, anyway—he and I didn't exactly have warm conversations about my day at work or my friends."

"What areas of the agency did you have access to while you were there?" China asked.

"All of them. As an administrative assistant, I was in a trusted position."

Not wanting to be the only one not asking questions, Myra jumped in with one of her own. "Could you hack into people's emails and things?"

I shook my head. "That would've been our technology people. The only computer I had access to was mine."

"But you did have access to all the offices," Ben mused.

"Over a year ago. And none of that matters now. I don't even know if the same people are working there."

"Maybe our guy number three doesn't know that," China said. "If Todd was desperate for money—which we suspect he must've been in order to cook up this wedding planner scheme—and if he was also trying to get back at you, he might've told guy number three that you still had access to the place, knew all the ins and outs, and maybe that you could even get into the safe or something."

"There wasn't a safe on the premises." I turned to Ben. "You said Harlow had other cards in his wallet. What were they?"

"A tax service, a bank, a dry cleaner, a construction company, a cell phone rep—"

"Wait a second," I said. "You said a construction company?"

"Yeah, why?"

"That could mean something. When the housing authority built new units, they'd accept bids from construction companies."

Mark sat up a little straighter. "And if you were on the inside—or knew someone on the inside—you could get a look at those bids so a construction company could undercut the competition."

"Right. I'll text my friend to see if the CHA is accepting bids on any construction projects." I got up and retrieved my phone from the kitchen.

"There's another angle we should consider here," said Ben. "The wedding planner might've killed Todd."

"But then who killed the wedding planner?" Myra asked.

"Guy number three," China chimed in from the ottoman. "My best bet is that Harlow and Todd were in cahoots. Guy number three killed them both. Now as to whether or not guy number three has left Brea Ridge or there's still something here he's after remains to be seen."

At that moment, it was like the four other heads in the room were on a timed swivel—they all turned to look at me.

CHAPTER TWELVE

Late that afternoon, it was down to just Ben and me. I was glad. We were lounging together on the sofa when our stomachs started grumbling.

"How about I make us some sandwiches?" I asked.

"Sounds good to me. I'll see if there are any good movies coming on."

I grinned. "At this point, I'd even settle for a bad one."

He kissed me. "I'll see what I can do."

I got up and went into the kitchen. I opened the refrigerator door and peered inside. "So what kind of sandwich would you like? We have ham, cheese, turkey, tuna, peanut butter—"

"Ham, please!"

I took out the ham, cheese, mayo, mustard, and pickles. I put all of that on the island and got the bread. Before I could get the bread out of the package, Mom and Violet came to the door.

"What a nice surprise!" And I really meant it.. I opened the door and gave them each a hug.

"Hello." Mom's voice being as stiff as a starched priest's collar should have been my first clue that all was not hunky-dory. "I'll go on into the living room and entertain Ben while you two talk."

Seeing that Mom had given my ex-husband my address so that he could come here and declare his love for me, I doubted my fiancé would find her very entertaining. But I was still trying to give everyone the benefit of doubt.

Mom went on into the living room, and Violet sat down on one of the stools at the island.

"Where's everyone else?" I asked.

"They went to dinner in Bristol."

"That's nice. Why didn't you and Mom go?"

"She wasn't feeling up to it." Her mouth tightened.

Clue number two.

"Oh. Would you care for a sandwich?" I went to the cabinet to get out plates.

"No, thank you. Mom is devastated that you're refusing to include her in your wedding."

I turned from the cabinet and gave Vi an exaggerated blink. "Excuse me?"

"You're letting Myra take over the wedding planning, and you aren't including Mom at all."

"Myra had already volunteered before Mom showed up, and Myra told her she could take part." I took two plates from the cabinet and slammed them onto the island. The fact that neither of the plates cracked or chipped spoke volumes about their durability.

"Oh, well, gee thanks, Myra, for throwing Mom a bone," said Violet.

"Look, the only reason Ben and I aren't eloping at this point is because you said your children would be hurt if they weren't included in my wedding. Here I thought you and Mom came to check on me. But, oh no! As usual, she's only concerned about herself! I thought you were better than that."

"Well, I'm so sorry that I take our mother's feelings into consideration!"

"She certainly took yours into consideration when she encouraged Todd to come visit your children without asking you first, didn't she?" I anchored my hands to my hips. If she wanted an argument, I was more than ready to give her one.

"That's not fair."

"No, it's not! Nothing about this week has been fair!" I began to pace, not wanting to look at her sickeningly sweet face while I spouted off injustices. "First, my oven—the source of my livelihood—breaks. Then my formerly incarcerated ex-husband shows up inside my house! But things are just getting interesting. Said ex-husband winds up murdered in his hotel room, and I get hauled down to the morgue to identify the body. I find out that my wedding planner—to whom I gave most of my savings—was a con man working with Todd. And, last but certainly not least, I learn that the wedding planner is dead and that my life might be in danger too." I whirled to face her. "Tell me where the fairness is in all that!"

She was sitting there on the stool, eyes wide and slack jawed. "Oh, Daphne, I didn't know." She got off the stool and held her arms open.

I put my outstretched arm between us. "Don't you dare touch me. I've been through the week from hell, you come over here to bless me out for not begging Mom to be my wedding planner, and now you want to hug and make up? Forget it. Get out of my house."

Tears spilled onto Violet's cheeks, and I turned away.

"I didn't know about the wedding planner working with Todd. Or that he was found murdered," she said. "Daphne, please—"

"You heard me. I'd like for you to leave." I went down the hall to the bedroom and slammed the door behind me.

A few minutes later, Ben came and lay down on the bed beside me. "Are you all right?"

I shook my head. He gathered me into his arms and held me while I wept.

* * *

Ben was still holding me when I awoke the next morning. We were both fully dressed, with the exception of our shoes. I gently disentangled myself and went to take a shower.

When I returned to the bedroom, he was just starting to stir. I sat on the edge of the bed, brushed his wavy hair away from his face, and kissed his forehead. His eyes opened.

I smiled. "Good morning."

"No fair. You're already sweet-smelling and dressed, and I look and feel like something somebody scraped off the bottom of his shoe."

"Didn't you hear my rant about fairness last night?" I laughed softly. "I imagine you're starving. I know I am."

"Tell you what. I'll go home, let Sally out, take a shower, and come take you to breakfast."

"I can make you a better deal than that. You go do all that, and I'll have breakfast ready when you get back."

He grinned. "That does sound like the better deal. I'll take it."

"And, hey, bring Sally back with you."

"You sure?"

"Positive," I said. "She and Sparrow have to start getting along sometime."

* * *

I fed Sparrow and explained to her that Ben would be returning with Sally. "I know you're not crazy about her, but you'll get used to her. And she'll get used to you. You're family now."

She didn't look up from her food. Was she merely eating, or was she ignoring me? Or both?

Knowing Sparrow, it was probably both. She typically did ignore me unless she was hungry or wanted to go outside. Lately, she had been humoring me by coming and rubbing against my legs in a just-here-to-say-hi gesture on occasion. It wasn't much. But given the fact that Sparrow had been a stray and had practically come with the house, I'd take what I could get.

I was on my way to wash my hands when the phone rang. It was Bonnie.

"Hey, girl," she said when I answered. "Sorry I didn't get back to you yesterday afternoon. I was swamped. So what's up?"

"I was wondering if CHA is currently accepting any construction bids."

She giggled. "Are you going into construction now?"

"No." I debated on how much to tell her. I decided I didn't have time to give her the full story, so I merely told her that I knew someone in construction and knew that CHA was often taking bids on new projects.

"Well, as a matter of fact, we are. So tell your friend to go on the website and get all the particulars on submitting a bid."

"Thanks. I'll do that."

"So how's the wedding coming along? Are you nervous?"

"You have no idea," I said. "I have finally started working on the wedding cake though."

"I'm sure it'll be beautiful and it'll taste good too."

I told her about the alternating chocolate and vanilla pound cake layers.

"And the dress? No, wait!" She stopped me before I could launch into a description. "Don't tell me. I want to be surprised. I'm so excited!"

"Me too. And I can hardly wait to see you. It seems like it's been forever."

"I know. Did you invite anybody else from work?"

"No, I didn't. You're the only person I've stayed in touch with."

"Aw, I'm special," she said. "That's so sweet. I haven't said anything to anyone else here because I didn't want to step on anyone's toes if you hadn't invited them."

She knew as well as I did that when the fiasco surrounding Todd's trial started, I was fair game for everyone—even my coworkers. Everyone wanted to talk with me about what it was like being shot at by my own husband, what I'd done to incur his wrath, what he'd been like prior to that evening, what it felt like to have your personal life splashed all over the local newspapers. Bonnie had been the only true friend I'd had in Tennessee during that whole situation.

We got ready to end our conversation, and she said she'd see me at the church next week.

"Whoa. Next week."

She giggled again. "Did that just dawn on you?"

"Yeah, I guess it did."

"Well, you try not to stress too much, and I'll look forward to seeing you then."

I ended the call and wondered about the church. When I'd sent out the invitations, I'd been certain I could book the church in plenty of time. But what if Myra hadn't been able to get it? I'd better call her and make sure.

A groggy Myra answered the phone. "'Lo?"

"Good morning. Did I wake you?"

"Humph. No, I'm awake." She yawned. "What's wrong?"

"My friend Bonnie from Tennessee called and mentioned the church. I just wanted to make sure we did get the church booked for next Saturday."

"We didn't."

"What?" My grip on the phone tightened.

"We're having the wedding in Belinda Fremont's garden." She yawned again. "She called and offered it last night. It'll be beautiful."

"Yes. Yes, it will. But what about all the guests with invitations telling them to go to the church?"

"We'll phone them. And put a sign on the church. I'll call you back in just a little while."

"Okay, Myra. Thank you."

"No prob, sweetie." She hung up. I was sure she had every intention of going back to sleep, and I was sorry I had awakened her in the first place.

I decided to make Ben some chocolate chip pancakes. As I got out the ingredients, I thought I should probably call Violet. Then I decided to wait until after breakfast. I felt that I owed her an apology for asking her to leave, but I was still stinging over the fact that she'd come to scold me for making our mother feel left out of the wedding plans.

I pinched the bridge of my nose. My mother was unbelievable. Not only had she thought I was being too hard on Todd when I'd divorced him from prison—she'd wanted me to drop the charges against him. But the charges had been filed by the state, and I'd had no control over them. Then she'd actually spoken with him over the phone and had given him my address! And she'd wanted him to spend time with her grandchildren—the ones he'd largely ignored for the majority of their lives? What was wrong with her?

The poor pancake batter bore the brunt of my frustration.

Ben returned with Sally as I was flipping the pancakes. He had the dog on a leash, and I was glad because otherwise she'd have jumped up on me and might've gotten too close to the stove.

"Wow. Those smell so good." He leaned against the counter. "What do you say Sally and I go get back in bed, and you bring us breakfast there?"

"I'd say dream on."

He laughed. "I'm glad to see you're feeling better this morning."

I didn't mention the fact that I'd already beaten the pancake batter into oblivion. "Well, I still need to call Violet and apologize for throwing her out of the house last night, but, hey, we're getting married at the Fremont mansion."

"We're what?"

I nodded. "I spoke with Myra, and Belinda Fremont has offered her garden to us as a wedding spot."

"But I thought we were getting married at the church."

"That's what I thought. And that's what our guests think." I grinned. "At this point, I've stopped questioning everything. I don't care when, where, or whether or not we have flowers. I just want to become Mrs. Ben Jacobs."

"And so you shall."

If I live to see next Saturday.

CHAPTER THIRTEEN

I t was a peaceful day. While Ben did some work on his laptop in the living room, I worked on the carved dog cake.

It was nice knowing he was there. I'd told him there was no need for him to "babysit" me. But he'd said Neil could hold down the fort for one more day—he was going to be managing the office while we were on our honeymoon.

Ben hadn't told me yet where we were going. He wanted it to be a surprise. That was probably a good thing. Had he left it up to me to plan the honeymoon, we'd probably wind up in a tent in my backyard given my luck with the wedding planner fiasco.

I'd started with the cake board. I covered it with a light blue gumpaste and then put a couple of white lines on the board to make it appear that the dog was sitting on a tiled floor.

I used cakes baked in two glass bowls—a four-cup and a two-cup—to make the dog's body. Once I got the two cakes put together and sufficiently carved to look like a dog's body, I transferred the cake to the cake board. I was covering the cakes in buttercream when Violet arrived. I stopped what I was doing, washed my hands, and answered the door.

Violet didn't come right on into the kitchen as she normally would have. "I came to apologize. Again. I'm sorry for yesterday."

I stepped onto the carport and hugged her. "I'm sorry too. Come on in." I looked past her to where she'd parked her car. "Are you alone?"

"Yes. Mom, Dad, Aunt Nancy, and Uncle Hal went home last night. They said they'd be back in a few days." She came on inside. "Of course, the kids are at day camp, so I'm getting ready to go into the office for a bit."

Violet was a real estate agent. In fact, she'd sold me my house.

"And Jason is at work," she continued.

There was still an awkward tension between us.

"I should never have asked you to leave yesterday," I said.

"No. You had every right to kick me out."

I winced at her choice of words. I mean, they were accurate but still painful. "I was just upset."

"I know. And I would've been too. Mom did step over the line in talking to Todd. I'd already taken that up with her, so I didn't beleaguer the point last night. Still, I didn't know about the wedding planner being in league with Todd."

"It's okay. It's like I told Ben last night: at this point, I don't even care about the wedding planning portion of the ceremony. I just want to marry him and get on with our lives."

"Here, here!" Ben called from the living room.

Violet laughed and stepped around the corner to say hello to him.

It was then that Neil arrived. He knocked on the door, causing Sally to come loping into the kitchen.

"Hi, Neil," I said opening the door. "Have you met Sally?"

"I haven't had the pleasure." He didn't pet the dog. "I'm on my lunch break, and I wanted to run something by Ben."

"Sure." I led him into the living room.

"Hey, Neil." Ben closed his laptop. "What's up?"

"What's up with you? Is that work you're doing?"

He shrugged. "Just trying to stay busy and keep out of Daphne's way. She has an important cake to deliver tomorrow."

"Oh. Well, I just want you to know that I have everything under control at the paper, so there's no need for you to stress over work."

"That's an excellent point," said Violet. "You don't need to be stressing about work either, Daph."

"Work is probably the only thing I'm not stressing over at this point."

"And I've always used work as one way to relax." Ben winked at me.

I blushed and smiled. I enjoyed his other relaxation techniques too.

"Well, I need to get to the office," Violet said. "Why don't you two come for dinner tonight?"

I glanced at Ben, and he gave me an almost imperceptible nod. "Sounds great. I'll bring dessert."

"Don't worry about dessert." She jerked her head toward the kitchen. "It looks like you've got your hands full with whatever that is you're working on in there."

"It's a dog. And I think I can still manage to bring a little something for the kids. If I don't, they'll be disappointed."

She laughed. "Yeah, and so will Jason. See you guys about six then."

As I was seeing her to the door, a young man in a brown pickup truck pulled into the driveway. Fortunately, he blocked Neil rather than Violet.

Still, she turned to me, putting her hand on my wrist. "Should I stay?"

"No. Ben and Neil are here. It'll be fine."

"Okay." She watched the man closely as he got out of the truck.

"How're you?" he asked her.

"Fine. You?"

"Finer than frog hair." He grinned.

Violet didn't smile back. She still looked concerned as she got into her car. I waved goodbye.

"Hi, I'm Daphne. What can I do for you?"

"I work with McElroy Haynes, and he sent me by here to make sure your oven's still working all right."

"It's doing great. Thanks."

"Are you using the oven at this time?" he asked.

"Not right this minute. But, believe me, it has been working great."

"Could I please come in and check the element with my meter? Mr. Haynes told me to, and I don't want to get on his bad side."

"All right." I opened the door. "Come on in."

"I'm Jeff, by the way." He brushed past me into the kitchen. "Would you please turn off the power to the oven through the breaker box?"

"Sure." I went down the hall to the breaker box and flipped the switch.

When I returned to the kitchen, Jeff was on his knees in front of my oven removing the heating element. "Mr. Haynes didn't tell me you have a dog."

"That's Sally."

I started to reiterate that the oven had been working perfectly fine, but I didn't bother. I supposed he knew what he was doing or that there was a reason that Mr. Haynes was afraid that the one he'd put in my oven was defective. I simply called Sally, and we went into the living room so the man could work.

Neil was leaving through the front door as I entered the room.

"The repairman will have to move his truck before you can leave, Neil. He has you blocked in." I returned to the kitchen and asked Jeff if he could move his truck.

Jeff—on his knees in front of my oven—fished into his pocket and dug out his keys. He pitched them to me. "You can move it."

"Thanks." I wasn't comfortable moving the man's truck, but I didn't want to hold Neil up. I went out and got into the truck. I started the engine and backed out of the driveway. Neil came out, waved, and got into his car.

As I waited for him to move, I glanced around the cab of the truck. Overall, it was neat. There were a few CDs stacked in the console tray, a now-warm half bottle of soda in one of the cup holders, and various business cards in another compartment of the console. One appeared to be for a landscaper, another for a construction company, and I could only see the tip of another that had a tree on the left side. I wondered if these were all people Jeff had come into contact with while working for McElroy Haynes or if maybe he was building a house.

Finally, Neil was on his way, and I was able to pull the truck back into the driveway. I went back inside and gave Jeff his keys.

I then went to the living room and sat on the sofa beside Ben. "Why did Neil come by?"

"He said he just came by to reassure me that he had things at the office handled." Ben jerked his head in the direction of the kitchen. "Trouble with the oven again?"

"No. He said Mr. Haynes sent him back to make sure the element was working properly."

"That seems odd."

I shrugged.

When Jeff got finished checking the heating element, he stuck his head into the living room. "Looking good, folks. Let us know if you have any more trouble."

"I will, Jeff. Thank you."

"Y'all have a nice one." He touched the brim of his cap and left.

"Now that Jeff is out of the kitchen, I'd better get back to the puppy dog."

"I'll go out and grab us some lunch," Ben said. "What would you like?"

"A deli sandwich would be super."

"Ham and Swiss on rye?"

I smiled. "You know me so well."

He gave me a kiss and strict instructions to keep the door locked until he returned. I put on my telephone headset and began mixing up a batch of rice cereal treats to use to form the dog's head. As I worked, I called Mom.

She must've seen it was me calling because she put on her long-suffering, self-pitying tone. "Hello."

Seriously, how she could convey so much melancholy with one word was beyond me. She should've been on the big screen.

"Hi, Mom. I'm calling to tell you that the venue for the wedding has been changed."

"Daphne?"

"Yes." Who else would it be?

"So I suppose Myra is responsible for this change?" she asked.

"If anyone is responsible, it would be me. I'm the one who hired the bogus wedding planner who failed to secure the church on the proper date. She did, however, acquire the new venue."

"And where's the ceremony taking place now?"

"In Belinda Fremont's garden."

"Belinda Fremont." Mom either paused for effect or because she really had to stop and remember where she'd heard the name. "Is that the eccentric, rich woman with the guinea pigs?"

"Yes, Mom."

In fact, I'd created a birthday cake for Belinda's prize-winning cavy Guinevere, and I'd catered the Fremont's New Year's Eve party too.

"The one who has an entire suite of her home dedicated to those...rodents?"

"That's right," I said. "I just hope Guinevere and her beau Lancelot don't decide to take Leslie's and Lucas's spots in the wedding."

"Please tell me you're joking."

"Of course, I'm joking. I think it's very generous for Belinda to offer her garden."

"Yes. That or she simply wants an excuse to show off that mansion of hers."

"Mom, Belinda doesn't need an excuse to show off her house. Besides, if I had a home like hers, I'd probably want to show it off too."

"Well, whatever." She sniffed. "I just wish you'd done a better job of investigating that wedding planner, and we wouldn't be having all these difficulties now."

"Oh, yeah. We certainly are having difficulties, aren't we? For your information, I called every reference Hunter Hampton—or Monty Harlow—gave me, and they seemed to check out."

"Naturally, they seemed to check out. They were in on the con."

I was gripping my cereal-mixing spoon so tightly that I had to make a conscious effort to loosen my grip. "Speaking of cons, why on earth would you give Todd my address and not only encourage him to visit me but to see Violet's family as well?"

"I thought it would be good for Todd. He sounded so bereft when we spoke," she said. "I've always felt that deep down he was a good man and that he loved you."

"That's because you're gullible. I have a good man who really does love me, and you nearly destroy it by sending my ex-husband to my door! Why didn't you at least warn me that he was coming?"

"I knew you'd refuse to hear him out unless he showed up unannounced and caught you off guard. You never want to listen to anyone else. You have your opinion, and you won't consider anyone else's."

"And you never think ahead. Why don't you consider consequences once in a while?"

"I will not be spoken to like this, Daphne. I'm finished talking with you."

I took a deep breath. "I hope to see you and Dad next Saturday."

"We'll see." With that, she hung up.

I dropped my spoon into my mixing bowl and went into the living room. I sat down on the sofa, and Sally came and put her head on my lap. I stroked her ears.

"Sally, I tried. I just wanted to call and tell her about the change of venue and try to smooth her ruffled feathers over allowing Myra to handle the wedding plans."

She raised her head and licked my nose.

"Thanks. I appreciate the gesture of support. But now I've got to face Violet this evening and let her know that I made things worse instead of better."

CHAPTER FOURTEEN

J ason greeted us at the door. He shook Ben's hand and hugged me. "How're you holding up?"

I looked around for the children.

"Don't worry," Jason said. "They're in the den playing video games."

"I'm okay, all things considered."

"Good." He turned to Ben. "I've reserved the party room at Dakota's for seven o'clock Friday evening for your bachelor party."

Dakota's was Brea Ridge's only steakhouse.

"Do you think we should still be having a bachelor party given everything that's happened?" Ben asked.

"Of course!" I said.

"Definitely!" Jason said simultaneously.

He and I smiled at each other. Neither of us wanted Todd's sudden appearance—and even more sudden death—to cast a pall over the wedding for Ben.

"You guys go ahead and talk bachelor party," I said. "I'll go find Violet."

"Kitchen," Jason said.

I took the box of cupcakes Ben had been holding and went to the kitchen. Violet was at the counter preparing a salad.

"Anything I can do to help?" I sat the box down.

"Nope. Just talk with me while I chop these carrots."

"I called Mom to tell her the location of the ceremony had been changed."

Violet stopped mid-chop. "I'm glad."

"Don't be. It didn't go well. I mean, I'd intended to make Mom feel included and wanted, but it blew up in my face. She asked about the wedding planner, and then I asked why she'd encouraged Todd to come here. It got ugly."

"I'll call her later tonight and try to smooth things over." Violet went back to chopping the carrots.

"No, that's okay. I think the more we discuss it, the worse it'll be. Just leave it alone for now."

She put the carrots into the salad and started on the cucumbers. "Are you sure?"

"Positive. Did you and Mom talk about the conversations she had with Todd?"

"We talked about them some."

"What did Todd say to Mom to make her believe he was so bereft?" I asked.

"He told her it was really hard for him on the outside. He said he'd lost his job, his friends, his standing in the community—and then he dropped the big heartwrencher—his wife."

"And whose fault was that?"

"I know, Daphne. I'm on your side, remember?"

I refrained from pointing out that it hadn't seemed like she was on my side last night.

"Mom offered Todd money and a place to stay if he'd go to Roanoke and start his life over there," Violet continued.

My jaw dropped. "She what?"

"I shouldn't have mentioned that. She was just concerned about him."

"This man shot at—and could've killed—me, and my own mother treats him like her son? She gave no thought whatsoever to me and my feelings."

Violet shushed her. "Please. I don't want Leslie and Lucas to hear. Todd simply played on her sympathies. He always could do that."

"I never understood why she liked him so much. She liked him better than she does me!"

"That's not true. She—"

"Aunt Daphne!" Leslie rushed into the kitchen and threw her arms around me. "I'm so glad you're here! Are you nervous about the wedding? You're going to look so beautiful."

"Aw, thanks, kiddo. You're the one who's going to look beautiful. And your mom is too."

"They'll look all right, but it's the bride's day to shine," said Lucas. "What's in the box?"

"Cupcakes."

He headed for his box, but his mother's voice stopped him in his tracks.

"Lucas Armstrong, don't even think about those cupcakes until after dinner."

"Well, that'll be hard to do because it's all I can think about now."

I laughed. "Who won the game?"

"We both did," said Leslie.

"It's a two-player game," Lucas explained. "You play as a team."

"Oh, that's good." I gave Violet a look of admiration.

"I've done this parenting thing for a while now. I've learned a few things."

* * *

When Ben and I returned to my house, we found a business card stuck in the door. It was in the side door, rather than the front door, so we figured it was someone we knew.

I took the card out of the door and turned it to the front. "Hunter Hampton, Wedding Planner."

"Let me see that." Ben examined the card, careful to hold it by the top and bottom so that he didn't further contaminate the card with his fingerprints.

"Do you think whoever killed Monty Harlow left that card here?"

"It's possible." He walked to the end of the carport and looked up the street. "Myra's home, and it looks as if Mark is with her. Let's head over there and call the police."

Myra and Mark were cuddled up on the sofa watching a movie when we arrived. They turned the movie off, and Myra got Ben a baggie to drop the business card in while I called the police station.

As we all sat around the living room waiting for the police, Bruno went from one of us to the other. He appeared to be excited to have so much company at once.

"Who do you think left the card?" Myra asked.

No one seemed inclined to answer, although the truth of the matter was right there in front of us all.

"It had to have been the person who killed Todd and Monty Harlow," I said. "Who else would have one of Hunter Hampton's business cards?"

She shuddered. "Well, I don't blame you a bit for not going inside. The killer might've been in there waiting for you."

"True," said Ben. "But I also didn't want to contaminate the door with more fingerprints. Hopefully, the police can get a print off the card or the door so that we can catch this guy and finally be done with this mess."

"I so want it behind us before the wedding."

Mark got up and looked out the window. "I had a friend hack into Todd's phone records. He was speaking with someone here in Brea Ridge on a regular basis for the past three weeks."

"It must've been Monty," I said. "That was about the time that Monty—or Hunter Hampton—became my wedding planner."

"Well, we know Monty didn't leave that card stuck in your door," said Mark. "The killer is sending you a message. He wants you to stay out of his way. You need to be extra careful, Daphne, until this guy is caught."

The deputy dispatched by the Brea Ridge Police Department was Officer Hayden. I'd met him not long after moving back home. He was a baby-faced man who looked like he'd just got out of high school and called me "ma'am." I knew he was actually much older than his appearance suggested and that he had a wife and child, but he didn't look intimidating in the least. I'd have preferred Officer McAfee. But, of course, beggars can't be choosers.

Officer Hayden came into the living room, got out a notebook, and took Ben's and my statement. It was the same statement. I felt that one of us should've been able to fill him in on what had occurred while we were on our way back to my house so that he could check and make sure no one was lurking in our home. After all, our pets were in there.

However, the officer wouldn't even let us accompany him until Ben mentioned that Sally was there and that she might bite him if he went in alone. Then he said he'd only let Ben go over with him, but Mark convinced him that he should go as well. I was told to stay with Myra.

As you might imagine, that didn't go over well with either of us.

"It's not as if you and I haven't thwarted our fair share of criminals." Myra gathered Bruno into her arms for a hug. "It's sexism; that's what it is. They think that because we're sexy, we can't defend ourselves. Well, I'll have them know, those detecting, fighting angels did a decent job of it. And so can we. I say we march our butts right on over there. Bill Hayden ain't the boss of us."

While I heartily agreed that Bill Hayden was not the boss of us, I wasn't about to let Myra put her life in danger. "I know, but I still think we should stay here. For the time being."

"Why?" She put Bruno onto the floor. "You need to be right there to see whatever it is they're finding. And so do I."

That was my angle. "True, but if I'm there and Hayden finds something unusual, he might say I planted it. The police are already suspicious of me in the deaths of Todd and Monty Harlow."

"That's nonsense."

"I know that, and you know that, but they're just trying to put somebody behind bars and wrap this case up."

"You've got a point." Myra opened the door and stepped out onto the porch. "Come on. We can at least peer over there and try to figure out what's going on."

I joined her on the porch. We sat on the steps and watched my house. We couldn't see much—only the lights coming on room by room.

"If Bill has to fire his sidearm, we might be able to see the flash," Myra said. "It probably depends on whether or not he fires it in the dark. If we see a flash like a gunshot in the darkness, we'll head over there."

"Okay." I prayed we would not see a gunshot flash.

It was then that China drove up. She pulled into Myra's driveway, cut her engine, and came to sit with us on the porch.

"Heard about what happened over the police scanner. I was going to go to Daphne's, but then I saw the two of you sitting here." She nodded her head toward the house. "Everything all right?"

"As far as we know, it is," I said.

"We're waiting for the menfolk to get back." Myra pretended she was holding a hand fan and fluttering it in front of her face. "You know we weak little ladies can't handle such excitement as a possible intruder."

"I've got the shotgun in the truck if you need it," China said. "But I'm guessing nobody is in there and that nothing in the house has been disturbed. I'm thinking the killer left that calling card to scare you, Daphne."

"It worked."

She patted my forearm. "I imagine it did."

"So what's your take on why this guy wants to scare Daphne?" Myra asked. "He's killed off his partners. Why doesn't he simply leave town? Why bother her?"

"Maybe he believes she still has something he wants," said China.

"Like what? Money?" I shook my head. "They took that."

"I wish I knew." The rest of China's thoughts were unspoken because we saw "the menfolk" heading back.

"Well? What'd you find?" Myra strode through the yard to meet the men. China and I stood, but we let them come to us.

"We didn't find anything," said Hayden. "I imagine that whoever left that card in your door did so to frighten you, Ms. Martin. We will check the card for fingerprints, but there weren't any on or around the door."

Ben put his arm around me. "And it doesn't appear that anyone went inside. The lock wasn't jimmied on the side door or the front door either. The windows were okay too. Everything looks fine."

"Sally and Sparrow are okay?" I asked.

He nodded. "They're great. Sally met us at the door, and Sparrow went running."

"They'd been in the same room then?"

"It appears so." He grinned. "They must be making progress."

"Must be."

"Ms. Martin, I'm heading back to the station now." Officer Hayden handed me his card. "Call us if you have any more trouble."

"Thank you. I will."

When he left, China once again offered her shotgun. "I'll be happy to leave it here for you if you think you'll need it.

It's got quite the recoil, but you don't have to be too awfully accurate for it to save your life."

"I'm afraid I might be in more danger with it than I would be without it," I said. "Still, I appreciate the offer."

"All right." She turned to Ben. "My friend Martha over at the paper says young Neil is sure feeling his oats. She said he's really looking forward to taking over in your absence."

"Yeah. I get the feeling he'd be happy to take over for me period. He was really hoping I'd take that job in Kentucky earlier this year and leave the editor position to him."

Ben had been approached—by an old flame, no less—to leave Brea Ridge and work for her start-up magazine in Kentucky. I was glad he turned down the offer...for more than one reason.

I hugged him tightly. "I, for one, feel that we're all right where we belong."

CHAPTER FIFTEEN

Monday morning over breakfast, I asked Ben what he'd be working on today.

"Well, Mark is following up on a lead about another of Todd's associates, and—"

"I'm talking about your Chronicle work," I interrupted.

"Oh, yeah, trust me. I have plenty I can do from here."

"You need to go into the office today, Ben. From what China said last night, I get the feeling that Neil is getting way too comfy in your chair."

"So what? He'll be running the paper next week anyway."

"And if you're out this week, he's running it now too. You need to go in and show your staff that you're still in charge."

"Are you trying to get rid of me?" He sipped his coffee and then put down his cup and smiled at me. "You're serious."

"I am. I don't know why, but I've got a bad feeling about him."

"Gee, I can remember a beautiful woman—she looked an awfully lot like you—telling me to give Neil more responsibility. 'You work too hard,' she said. 'Trust Neil to do his job so that you can take more time off,' she said." He frowned. "I could've sworn that was you, come to think of it."

"That was different. That was when you were working yourself to death and not letting anyone help you at all." I huffed. "That was when you didn't feel it was necessary to be my bodyguard."

"I like guarding your body." He gave me an appraising look. "It's a great body."

"You're trying to get me off track. I'll be fine. Please go into the office today."

"You were just threatened again last night. Do you honestly think I'm going to leave you?"

"I wasn't threatened," I said. "Not really. Would it make you feel better if I called China and asked her to bring over her shotgun?"

"Um…no, it would not." He sighed. "All right. I'll go in— for a little while. Promise me you won't open the door for anyone and that you'll call me if you need me."

I got up, went around to the back of his chair, and slid my arms down his chest. "I'll need you." I kissed his neck. "I always need you. But I'll just have to wait until you get home."

"Keep that up, and I won't go anywhere."

* * *

I'd just put two tiers of our wedding cake into the oven— the ten-inch and six-inch chocolate layers—when there was a knock at the side door.

I went to the door and immediately recognized Jeff, the young man who worked for McElroy Haynes. I opened the main door but left the storm door closed and locked.

"Hi. Don't tell me Mr. Haynes sent you back to check that element again."

He smiled. "No, ma'am."

"Well, that's good because I'm using the oven right now."

"Like I said, that's not why I'm here this morning."

"Why are you here?"

"I came to ask you on a date," he said.

I thought that was ridiculous—the man was at least ten years younger than me. As he stood there with his aw, shucks persona, I wondered if there could be more to Jeff than met the eye.

"You didn't happen to come by here last night, did you?"

"No. Why?"

"Someone stopped by and left a business card in my door."

Jeff frowned. "I didn't know McElroy even had business cards."

"Oh, it wasn't Mr. Haynes' card," I said. "It was a card from...someplace else."

"Well, I do a little moonlighting here and there, but none of the places I work for have fancy cards." He smiled again. "So, what do you say?"

"To what?"

"To the date. Dang, you're pretty but a tad slow."

"I don't think my fiancé would appreciate my going out with another guy." I laughed. "In fact, I'd better let you be on your way. I need to check on our wedding cake—that's what's in the oven."

"Oh, well. Congratulations." He turned and left.

I closed the main door and locked it. I realized my hands were trembling, and I went into the living room and sank onto the sofa. That young man was probably harmless, but I was looking for murderers around every corner.

* * *

I'd gotten the cakes out of the oven and had put them on wire racks to cool. I had one tier left—the eight-inch vanilla—and I'd bake it tomorrow.

I went into the office and booted up the computer to look for ideas on decorating the cake table. As a decorator, I was used to concentrating on the cakes. The only time I'd really prepared a cake table display was for the cake competition I'd taken part in this past spring. Typically, I designed the cake, and the caterer or event planner took care of the display.

There was the beautiful white cake stand I'd already planned to use. Plus, I could drape the table with dark pink tulle and a white lace underskirt. But I wanted a little more oomph.

Scrolling through the images I'd located through a search engine, I saw that some people put photographs of themselves or their parents on the table. That was a nice touch, but I didn't know how big the cake table was going to be. I needed to check with Myra or Belinda on that.

Another display I particularly liked had a glass top for the cake with roses and orchids between the glass and rest of the table. I could do something like that. I doubt I could afford the orchids, but white and pink roses would be beautiful.

A message popped up telling me I had a new email. I checked my inbox and found that the message was from Bonnie.

Are you stressing out? You sounded a little on edge when I spoke with you the other day, and I just want to make sure you're all right.

Rather than respond in writing, I gave her a call. I realized she was at work, but I wouldn't keep her long.

"Chilton Housing Authority, Bonnie speaking."

"Hey! It's Daphne. I just got your email and wanted to hear your voice."

"Is everything okay? You sounded stressed the other day."

"Believe me, I have been stressed." I told her about first finding Todd in my kitchen and then learning that he'd been murdered.

"Murdered? Oh, my gosh. That's terrible."

"I know. And I had to identify him for the police."

"Oh, Daphne. I'm so sorry."

"Thanks. I just need to put it behind me. But I wanted you to know why it sounded like I was freaking out when you called."

"It's because you were," she said. "I've been debating on whether or not to tell you this, but Todd contacted me a couple of weeks after he got out of prison."

"He did what?" Her revelation made me lightheaded. Why hadn't she contacted me as soon as this happened? Why had she kept this from me?

"I didn't even know who he was when the receptionist asked to put a call through from Todd Martin. I thought he was a loan client or something. And then he explained everything to me."

"Explained everything?" I imagine I sounded like a parrot, but I was so floored that I didn't know what to say.

"He told me he was your ex-husband—actually, he said that at about the same time that I made the connection myself—and asked if I knew where you were living now," said Bonnie. "I told him that the last I heard, you'd moved to somewhere in Virginia."

I breathed a little easier. At least she hadn't told him I was in Brea Ridge. Of course, Mom had taken care of that.

"He started going on about how he wanted to make everything up to you," she continued. "He even told me about getting down on one knee and proposing to you with his grandmother's engagement ring. He said it was the best night of his life. I didn't buy it, though, and I merely wished him luck on his quest."

"Why didn't you say anything to me about this before?"

"I didn't want to upset you. I knew you and Ben were getting married soon and that the last thing you wanted was for Todd to come back around and try to ruin everything." She paused. "I'm sorry. I guess I should've called and warned you that he was looking for you."

I was silent while I digested what she'd said. His grandmother's engagement ring. Could that be what Todd had been looking for? I had no idea what it was worth. And Todd hadn't talked as if he'd been particularly close to his grandmother. But I'd sent that ring to his mother via certified mail after we'd divorced. How did he not know that?

"Are you angry?" Bonnie asked.

"No. I'm just trying to figure out what it was Todd really wanted. He didn't contact me in all the years that we were apart—not once. And then he came here to Brea Ridge trying to act like he loved me and wanted to get back together. I knew that was fishy from the start. And I think I know now why he was here."

"Why?"

"To get his grandmother's engagement ring," I said. "He'd been talking to Mom and crying hard times to her. She even offered to help him relocate in Roanoke."

"What?" Bonnie's voice reached a volume and pitch that seared through my brain.

"Yeah, well—anyway, I think now that he needed money and wanted to pawn that ring. But I returned it to his mother years ago."

"Too bad he didn't know that before coming to Brea Ridge. What do you think got him killed?"

"I believe he must've gotten mixed up with some criminals—either while he was still in prison or as soon as he got out," I said. "It's possible he owed one of them money. But, then, why would they kill him? All the cop shows say criminals don't kill someone who owes them money because dead people don't pay."

"Maybe he wasn't trying to get money to pay back to someone he owed. Maybe he was going to use it to try to start a new life somewhere—somewhere other than your mom's neighborhood."

* * *

After talking with Bonnie, I called Myra.

"Do you know what color table linens we'll be using for the reception?" I asked.

"Belinda said she'd have her staff simply use what they always used for garden parties—white linen tablecloths and napkins. Is that all right?"

"That's great. For the wedding cake display table, I'd like to have a smaller table just to highlight the cake. We'll have the cake, the server, two small plates, and napkins for Ben and me to use after we cut the cake and feed bites to each other."

"Okay. What else do you need?"

"I want a white lace tablecloth, and then I want to drape the table in dark pink tulle. You think we can get those at a craft store in Bristol or Kingsport?" I mentioned my idea of having a separate glass tabletop with flowers beneath it. "Do you think we can do that?"

"I'm sure we can. Maybe we can head out to the craft stores tomorrow."

"Good. And I'll need to call Steve Franklin," I said. "He told me he could help me get the flowers at wholesale price, and I also want to put pink and white roses beneath the glass."

"That'll be beautiful." Myra giggled. "I'm so excited."

"Me too." I'd said that to Leslie, but this time it was truer. I was starting to get excited about the wedding again. It would be wonderful to put all this business with Todd behind me and move forward with my life.

"By the way, did you know that Monty Larson had a girlfriend?"

"No." I scoffed. "I guess she was supposed to have been my pianist?"

Myra laughed. "Probably. Or, more likely, your kazoo player."

"I cannot believe I was so taken in by that man."

"Now, don't worry about that. The past is the past. Let's move forward. The only reason I told you about the girlfriend is because she's still here."

"Here?" I exclaimed. "In Brea Ridge? I need to talk with her!"

"Actually, Mark is on his way to do just that."

"You and I need to talk with her too, Myra. Where is she?"

She was quiet long enough for me to realize that she was debating whether or not she should tell me.

"You know that you and I can reach her better than Mark can," I said. "I mean, I realize Mark is a wonderful interrogator, but he's still a man. She'll identify better with the two of us."

"That's exactly what I told him when I tried to get him to take me with him in the first place. He said it might be dangerous and that I should stay here."

"But it won't be dangerous if both of us are there." I knew it wouldn't take much to push Myra over the edge. "Am I right?"

"You're absolutely right. He's buying her a cup of coffee at that little diner in town. You want to drive, or you want me to?"

"I'll drive," I said, already getting my purse and keys and heading for the door. "I'll be to get you in about two minutes."

CHAPTER SIXTEEN

"It's a good thing for me that you're slipping," I told Myra on the drive to the diner. "If not, you'd have gone with Mark in the first place, and I wouldn't have even known about this visit with Monty's girlfriend."

"I am most certainly not slipping. If I'd gone with Mark, I'd have missed the last fifteen minutes of The Young and the Restless, and it was an exciting episode. Besides, I get some of my best detecting tips from Paul Williams."

Paul was one of Myra's favorite characters on the soap opera. He'd been on the show and been portrayed by the same actor for more than thirty-five years.

"I know, I know. I just hope we're not too late to get in on this interrogation," I said.

"We won't be." Myra took a compact from her purse and powdered her face. "I don't know how much this woman will be able to tell us."

"Neither do I, but I don't want to miss any of it."

The diner wasn't terribly busy at this time of day, so I found a parking spot easily. When we walked inside, Mark's eyes widened in a what-are-you-two-doing-here expression that both Myra and I ignored.

The pair was seated at a booth. We joined them—Myra sliding onto the bench beside Mark while I sat with Monty's girlfriend.

"Hi." Myra reached across the table to offer her hand to the mousy young woman. "I'm Myra Jenkins."

The girlfriend shook Myra's hand. "I'm Lila Canter."

"Nice to meet you."

"I'm Daphne Martin." I decided to forego the handshake. "I'm Todd's ex-wife. Did you know Todd?"

Lila nodded. "He was friends with Monty."

Mark cleared his throat. "Lila and I were in the middle of a conversation."

"Would you please bring us up to speed, darling?" Myra asked, tilting her head to give her beloved a sidelong glance and coquettish smile.

I'd have to ask her if she'd watched Gone with the Wind lately because that was a Scarlett O'Hara move if I'd ever seen one.

Mark made a noise that was somewhere between a sigh and a growl. "Lila began seeing Monty when he got out of prison a few months ago."

"Honey, wasn't he a little old for you?" Myra asked.

Lila twirled her lank brown hair around her forefinger. "Maybe a little. But he was nice to me. And he had big plans that he wanted to include me in."

"Plans like swindling a woman out of the majority of her savings?" I asked.

"Todd told us you were mean." She raised her chin. "He said you put him in prison and then divorced him."

"I didn't put him in prison. He shot a gun at me, and the state prosecuted him for it." I stopped when I saw the waitress approaching.

Myra and I both ordered soft drinks.

After the waitress hurried off to get our drinks, I continued. "So, basically, Todd put himself in prison. Did he tell you anything about the night he took a shot at me?"

Lila shook her head and looked down at the table.

"This is why it's best that I talk with Lila alone," Mark said. "You're upset, Daphne, and you're upsetting her. You need to understand that Lila has been through an ordeal herself. Her boyfriend was murdered."

I took a deep breath and tried to refocus. "I realize that. And I'm sorry for your loss, Lila. I just want—we just want—to try to figure this whole thing out and help the police catch whoever is responsible for Monty's and Todd's murders."

"I want that too," she said.

The waitress returned with our drinks—new ones for Myra and me and refills for Lila and Mark. "Let me know if y'all need anything else."

Mark moved his straw from his nearly empty glass to the full one. "Now that we've established that we all have the same goal, could I please continue speaking with Lila?"

"May we stay?" I asked.

He drew his bushy eyebrows together as he considered my request.

"We promise to be quiet," Myra said.

I knew that was a promise neither of us would be able to keep, but it worked.

"Fine. Just let me and Lila do the talking." He sipped his cola before addressing Lila. "Whose idea was the wedding planner scheme?"

"It was Todd's. See, after Todd got out of prison, he got really frustrated at not being able to find a good-paying job. Monty was upset about that too. So one night they got to talking over beers. Monty had a friend who sold stolen merchandise. The friend's boss was looking for some more help because he'd robbed a warehouse the week before."

I wanted to grab this girl—who couldn't have been more than twenty-five—by the shoulders and ask her what in the world was wrong with her. How did she get mixed up with a criminal like Monty Harlow and believe that staying in a relationship with him was a good idea?

"I take it Monty and Todd decided to sell stolen merchandise for the friend's boss," Mark said. "What kind of merchandise was it?"

Lila raised and dropped one bony shoulder. "Some kind of electronic stuff or something. I don't know."

"How did that turn out?" he asked.

"Not good. The boss accused them of shorting him somehow. They swore they didn't, but it was their word against his, and he had a bunch of guys backing him." She went back to playing with her hair. "They paid him whatever he said they owed him. But then one of his crew saw Monty with his parole officer, and the boss started thinking that maybe Monty and Todd were informants for the police."

"That's not good," Myra said. "That's the sorta thing that gets you whacked."

Mark leveled his gaze at her.

"Well, it is!" She grimaced. "Sorry, Lila. Please go on."

"The guys knew they needed to get out of Tennessee, so they started coming up with ways to get money. Monty's family has pretty much disowned him, but Todd called around to some old family members and friends." She looked at me. "When he found out you were getting married, he and Monty cooked up the wedding planner scheme."

"And that's what brought Monty to Brea Ridge," Mark said.

"Monty and Todd too. Todd actually stayed in Abingdon the whole time because he didn't want to be seen by Daphne or anyone else who might know him." She took a drink of her soda. "But he'd been here the whole time. The money from the wedding planner business and what Todd could make by selling some sort of ring was supposed to have bought us all new identities and helped us get somewhere that we could start new lives." She dropped her chin. "Monty was going to marry me."

I put my hands in my lap so I could clench them without anyone knowing it. This idiotic girl! The wedding planner business? It wasn't a business! It was a con—a con to screw me out of my savings!

"Lila, do you think the crime boss from Tennessee either came here or sent someone here to murder Todd and Monty?" Mark asked.

"I don't think so. We'd all been careful. We kept an eye out for guys we knew were in the crew and for people who looked like they didn't belong around here." She sighed. "I believe that whoever they got involved with after they got here killed them."

That nearly brought me up out of my seat. "What? What do you mean—whoever they got involved with after they got here?"

Again, Lila lifted and dropped one shoulder. "I'm pretty sure they were running some other racket from here, one I didn't know about. They met somebody somewhere in Bristol once or twice a week almost from the time we got into town. When I asked Monty about it, he got angry and said that Todd was being stupid and getting distracted. He said this wasn't in their original plan and that they needed to stay on track."

"And you don't know who or where they were meeting?" Mark asked her.

"No. But I'm pretty sure it had something to do with her." Lila flicked a hostile gaze in my direction. "Todd was really mad about her getting married. Monty was like, who cares, let's get our money and run. But Todd wanted something else."

"He wanted to hurt me," I said softly.

"Yeah. I guess so."

* * *

After talking with Lila, Mark offered to drive Myra back home. I was glad. I needed to be alone. Rather than going straight home, I drove. It was a beautiful sunny day, and the curvy, mostly deserted roads allowed me to be alone with my thoughts.

I remembered how it had been to be Todd's wife. Some days it seemed that everything I did made him angry. I was either "questioning his authority" or "acting like I was smarter than he was." That was in addition to the accusation that I was seeing someone behind his back. I don't know how I could've ever seen anyone behind his back. He checked the mileage on my car daily.

But when I made him angry enough to punish me but not angry enough to physically hurt me, he'd lash out at me emotionally or psychologically. The fact that he'd been behind the wedding planner scheme—something I'd already guessed but that Lila confirmed—was proof that Todd not only wanted to hurt me financially, he'd wanted to ruin my wedding. It was likely that he'd also planned to ruin my relationship with Ben.

I could see Todd's twisted logic in this. He'd served his time in prison and couldn't even get a well-paying job. I, on the other hand, had moved back to Brea Ridge and had stared a whole new life—a better life—and it was going well. Naturally, he'd want to ruin all of that if he could.

Plus, he would still see me as his property. I'd been his to control and manipulate. I imagined he got a kick out of knowing that he was doing that again through Monty Harlow. But who was he seeing in Brea Ridge, and why? Lila said she felt sure it had something to do with me. The cold chill snaking down my spine told me she was right.

I turned the car around and headed back into town. I needed to talk with Violet. I called her cell and learned that she was at the office. I said I'd be there soon.

When I got there, she had clients in her office. I sat down in the lobby to wait, but then I stood and began to pace. She didn't keep a receptionist during the summer since her hours were irregular, so there was no one to talk with to help me keep my mind occupied.

I looked out the window at the breeze ruffling the leaves of the maple trees. There was the red and white sign that Jason had touched up three weekends ago, "Violet Armstrong, Licensed Realtor." Pink and white impatiens covered the ground around the base of the sign.

Thoughts of Todd's face flooded my mind: angry, taunting, sneering, hard as granite. I resumed pacing and tried to replace those memories with images of Ben, but it was tough when I needed desperately to know who Todd had been scheming with here in Brea Ridge.

At last, Violet saw her clients to the door, thanked them for stopping by, and told them she'd be calling them soon with some new listings.

As they walked down the steps, she turned to me and her smile disappeared. "You're as white as a sheet. What's wrong?"

I explained about the meeting with Monty Harlow's girlfriend. "She says there was someone here in Brea Ridge who was working with Todd and Monty. She didn't know what they were up to, but she said it involved me."

Violet put her hand on my back and directed me into her office. I went inside and sat down, and she closed the door.

Sitting on the chair beside me, she said, "Did she have any idea who this other person was?"

"Apparently not. I'd love for you to talk with Mom and very casually ask exactly what she and Todd said to each other."

"You honestly don't think Mom was involved in some sort of plan with Todd, do you?"

I spread my hands. "She did invite him to Roanoke to start over there." Before Violet could protest, I hurried on. "But, no, I don't think she was the person meeting with him and Monty once or twice a week. That was someone who lived here, and I need to find out what the three of them were up to."

"Why don't you call Mom yourself and hash this out with her?"

"She likes you best."

"Daphne!"

"She does. Besides, every time I talk with her, I wind up making matters worse."

Violet nodded. She couldn't deny that truth. "I haven't had time to talk with her since y'all had your latest blow-up, so I can use that as an excuse to call. Then I'll find out precisely what she and Todd talked about when he called her."

"Do you think he called her more than once?"

"I don't know, but I'll ask. I'll also see if he mentioned any Brea Ridge associates he was hanging out with while he was in town."

"I didn't even know he had Brea Ridge associates," I said. "We moved to Tennessee as soon as we got married, and he wasn't from here originally. How could he have any friends or contacts in this little Podunk town?"

"UT is a huge regional college. If he had any Brea Ridge connections, I'm sure they were people he met in college."

"Excellent point." I was struck again about how his years at college had seemed to have been the best, most important time in Todd's life. "While you're getting information from Mom, I'll try to find a list of University of Tennessee alumni now residing in Brea Ridge."

CHAPTER SEVENTEEN

I drove home and went straight to my office. I booted up the computer and found the URL of the University of Tennessee website. In order to search alumni information, I had to register. Since I didn't want the search traced back to me, I registered as Todd Martin.

You'd think I'd have been familiar with the same people as Todd. But although we met in college, we didn't run in the same circles. Plus, if the person he was plotting with had been a graduate of UT, he—or she—could have been at the school at any time, not just the same time period as Todd.

I felt as if I were grasping at straws. Still, doing an alumni search made me feel as if I was at least trying to connect the dots between someone here in Brea Ridge—other than me—and Todd.

The directory began to load. I refined my search to alumni currently living in the region of Brea Ridge, Virginia. That narrowed the field down considerably.

Steve Franklin. Hmm. I hadn't realized Steve had gone to UT. I'd been under the impression that he'd graduated from a Virginia college. His graduation date wasn't listed.

Neil Grant. That was Ben's editorial assistant. He'd graduated in 2007—ten years after Todd and me.

Those were the only two names I recognized. There were a couple of other people from Brea Ridge and quite a few from Abingdon and Bristol, but I saw nothing that would make me think any of them had a connection to Todd.

I opened a new tab and took a look at my website. It could use an update. I had made and photographed several cakes that weren't on the site and needed to be uploaded to the gallery. The phone rang, and I decided my site update could wait until after the wedding. It was Violet.

"What did you learn from looking at the UT alumni directory?" she asked.

"Nothing really, except that Steve Franklin and Neil Grant went there."

"Do you think either of them was in cahoots with Todd?"

I chuckled. "Doubtful. Steve wouldn't want to lose his only bakery provider, unless he has someone else in mind for the job. And Neil wouldn't want anything interfering with my marriage to Ben because he really wants Ben out of the office so he can be in charge for a while."

"Well, that's no good."

"Did you talk with Mom?" I asked.

"Yeah. She really felt sorry for Todd when he called her. He apparently tugged on her heartstrings pretty hard. That's why she offered to help him start over in Roanoke."

The fact that she did that still made me furious, but I didn't say anything.

"He mentioned his grandmother's engagement ring to Mom," Violet continued. "She told him she didn't know if you still had it or not. Didn't you tell her you returned it?"

"No." I blew out a breath. "Mom and I had argued and become really distant after I served Todd with divorce papers, and I…I wasn't talking with her at that time."

"Oh." She paused, as if she was scrambling for something to say. "Maybe Mom was reaching out to Todd to find out more about what had gone on between the two of you. You know he always behaved like a model citizen around us. Maybe she wanted to feel him out—have him tell her whether the abuse had been ongoing or a one-time thing."

"I could have told her if she'd have ever asked me."

"She never asked?" Violet sounded confused.

"Not really. After the shooting incident and after I told her I was divorcing Todd, she told me I was being unreasonable. I said she didn't know what it was like."

"And she didn't press you? She didn't want you to tell her what it was like?"

"No." I replayed the conversation over in my head.

"Maybe she wasn't ready to hear the truth. I know I wasn't. When I found out what you'd been going through with Todd all those years, I was devastated." Her voice broke. "How could I have not known? How had I not seen any warning signs?"

"Vi, we lived two hundred and fifty miles away from each other. And I hid the truth about my life so well that not even the people I worked with suspected that we weren't your typical happy couple."

"I just wish you'd have told me. Jason and I would've come down there and brought you home."

Tears pricked my eyes and made my nose burn. "Stop before you have me crying. It happened. It's over and done with. And I'm moving on with my life."

"I know. You're right." She sniffled, and it was like a jab to my heart. "I love you."

"I love you. And I'm going to try again to clear the air with Mom. Maybe if she hears—from me—a tiny bit of what my life was like with Todd, she'll be happy for Ben and me."

"Honey, she is happy for you. Or at least, she wants you to be happy. I just think she honestly couldn't get her mind around the fact that Todd wasn't the person he presented to her and Dad."

"Yeah. I guess."

After talking with Violet, I took a deep breath and then I...ate a fudge brownie. Hey, a girl needs a shot of courage in the form of chocolate once in a while, doesn't she?

I dialed Mom's number, half hoping she wouldn't pick up.

"Hello."

Dread made me hesitate.

"Hello?" she repeated.

"Hi, Mom. It's me."

"Daphne, what's wrong?"

"Nothing. Everything's fine."

"You don't sound as if everything's fine," she said.

"I just wanted to clear the air between us."

"Oh." Her tone instantly became guarded.

"I didn't call to argue." Was I being reassuring or merely making matters worse? "I spoke with Violet, and she said she felt as if you couldn't quite correlate the Todd you know with the Todd I lived with for fifteen years."

"Well, that's true. Todd always came across as mannerly and kind to your dad and me. And he seemed so protective of you. Whenever I'd call and you were out, Todd knew exactly where you were and what you were doing."

"That's because I had to get his permission if I wanted to go anywhere," I said.

"A husband wanting to be apprised of his wife's whereabouts doesn't mean he's demanding permission,

Daphne. It means he's asking you to be considerate. Didn't you want to know where he was when he was out?"

I clenched my fist. "It wasn't like that. If I asked where he was going and when he was coming back, it was none of my business. But when I went less than a mile out of my way on the way home from work to visit a bookstore, Todd shot a gun at me."

"That was what you did? You just went to a bookstore?"

"Yes."

"A regular old bookstore?" she asked.

"Yes."

"Had you dated someone who worked there or something?"

"Mom, how can you not know the reason my husband shot at me?" My mind added, Are you really so dense?

"You said you'd taken a detour on your way home from work. I simply thought it had to be something...well, something else."

"I know you believe I deserved the treatment I received from Todd, but I didn't," I said. "It took me a long time and two therapists to come to that conclusion, but I finally did. Normal couples don't give one partner complete control over their finances. They don't go to work and come straight home without ever doing anything fun together. Or by themselves, for that matter. Normal couples go out to dinner, go to movies, go on vacations, go hiking. They have picnics and snowball fights."

"You didn't?"

"No." My voice sounded small and weak when I spoke again. I didn't like sounding that way, but I couldn't make my voice any better at the time. "You know how you always bragged about how well I kept the house? If I didn't keep it clean and organized, I was punished. I was forced to quit my pastry class at the community college because Todd thought I might be having an affair with the instructor. He was even jealous of a neighbor's son who used to visit, and he refused to let me see him again."

"How old was this neighbor's son?"

"He was eleven, Mom. He saw in me someone as lonely as he was. We became friends. He started coming over one summer when I was off and Todd was at work, and we'd play board games or cards on the front porch. One day, Todd came home early. He was nice to the kid, but I told him he should go on home because I needed to make dinner..." I trailed off.

"And then what happened?"

"Todd broke my pinkie and dared me to associate with the boy again," I said. "He broke the pinkie rather than another finger because I could still work with a broken pinkie. Having to shun the boy hurt worse than the broken finger, though. He didn't have many friends, and he couldn't understand why I'd deserted him."

I didn't mention it to Mom, but it was in the next few months that Todd shot me. When the boy had seen the story on the news, he and his mother had come to visit. The boy had said, "I knew he was mean to you. That's why he didn't let you be my friend anymore. He didn't want you to have anyone but him."

Out of the mouths of babes.

"I'm sorry. Why didn't you tell us?"

"I was afraid that you and Dad would simply see it as one more failure on my part."

"One more failure?" she asked. "What are you talking about? When did we ever call you a failure?"

"You never called me a failure, Mom. You didn't have to. It was obvious that Violet was the golden child. She won Miss Brea Ridge. She got married to a man with an excellent job. She gave you beautiful twin grandchildren."

"We were proud of you too," Mom said.

"For what? I did absolutely nothing out of the ordinary."

"You are anything but ordinary. You are beautiful and smart and talented. And strong. I always wished I could be as strong as you."

I barked out a laugh. "Oh, yeah. I was so strong that my husband had to shoot at me and be removed from our home by sheriff's deputies before I could muster up the courage to leave him. I was so empowered that I couldn't divorce the man until he'd been sentenced to prison."

"You were strong. You are strong. I'm sorry your dad and I never knew what you were going through. I wish you'd have trusted us enough to confide in us."

"It wasn't a matter of trust, Mom. After the first few months, he had me convinced that I deserved the treatment I given because I was ugly and stupid and immature and irresponsible. On some level, I knew that wasn't true. But when those things are hammered into your head over and over, you can't help but start believing them."

"Oh, Daphne." She started to cry.

"Please. It's all right."

"It's not all right! I offered to help that monster make a new start! How could I do such a thing?"

"You didn't know." My own tears blurred my vision.

"I wish I could take it all back."

"It's time to start over," I said. "I'm getting ready to start a new life with Ben. We can all move forward together."

"Okay. We will. And if he ever mistreats you, you'll tell us?"

I laughed. "I won't have to. I've had therapy now. I'd tell him to hit the road and keep bouncing."

Mom laughed too. "You sounded like your grandmother when you said that."

"But he won't abuse me. Ben is good to me. He truly loves me, and I love him."

"Yeah." She sniffled. "Everything will be better this time."

"Yes. It will."

* * *

I called Violet back to let her know that my talk with Mom had gone well. "I feel like we've really turned a page."

"That's good."

"What's wrong? You sound distracted."

"It's nothing. Lucas' and Leslie's bus bringing them home from day camp is running late today. They're actually fifteen minutes late already, and I'm getting worried."

"Have you called the day camp?" I asked.

"Yeah. There was no answer."

"They'll be home soon." But with everything that had happened within the past few days, I couldn't help but share her concern.

CHAPTER EIGHTEEN

After instructing Violet to stay at home and to call me when the kids got there safely, I went to the church where they were attending day camp. No one was there. There were no cars in the parking lot, and the church bus wasn't there either.

Still, I went to the door to see if maybe there was still someone inside cleaning up or something. I tried the door, but it was locked. I knocked, but there was no answer. I went around to the side of the building and tried another door. No luck.

I got back into my car and began driving the route the church bus would have taken to drive Leslie and Lucas home. Of course, there would have been other children to drop off, so I couldn't be sure the exact route the bus would take. But I thought taking the direct route from the church to Violet's house would be a good place to start.

I was halfway to Violet's house when she called me. She was weeping and trying to talk. I pulled over to the side of the road.

"Violet! Calm down! Tell me what's wrong!"

"Th-they...they're...k-kidnapped."

"What? No. That can't be."

"J-just...got...a call." She cried out with a moan of frustration and horror.

"Sit tight. I'm on my way. They're okay, Vi."

The first person I called was Jason.

"What?" That he answered with one word and a clipped tone told me he already knew what was going on.

"Have you called the police?" I asked.

"Yes. They're meeting us at the house."

"I'll be there as soon as I can. Everything will be fine." The platitude sounded as hollow as the one I'd told my sister.

I called Ben.

"Hey, babe. What's up?"

Hearing his sweet voice was the last straw for me. I began weeping.

"Daphne, what's going on? Where are you?"

"I'm on the side of the road."

"Have you wrecked?"

"N-no." I took a deep, shuddering breath. "I was out looking for the bus from day camp. Lucas and Leslie are missing. Violet said…" Another whimper. "They've been kidnapped."

"I'm on my way to you. Don't drive."

"I have to drive. I'm almost to Violet's house. I'll be fine."

"I'm on my way," he said. "Have the police been notified?"

"Yes."

"Daphne, please be careful."

* * *

Why on earth would someone kidnap Leslie and Lucas? That's the question I asked myself over and over as I continued driving to Violet's house. She and Jason seemed to be doing all right financially, but they weren't the type of rich people whose children got ransomed for huge sums. It had to be something else.

When I arrived at the house, the police were asking the same questions I'd been asking myself on the drive over. Both Officers McAfee and Hayden were standing in the living room. Hayden was talking with Violet, and McAfee was talking with Jason.

"When he called, he only said he had the children. He said he'd call back soon with instructions," my sister was saying through her tears. "He has my babies!"

"We know, Violet," said Officer Hayden. I remembered that the Hayden children went to school with Lucas and Leslie. "We'll get them back."

I'd never felt more helpless in my life. I went to her and put my arm around her shoulders. She turned and clung to me as she sobbed.

"Please." My eyes bore into Hayden's. "What can we do?"

"We've put out an Amber Alert, so Lucas' and Leslie's photographs will be all over the news and social media. We've blocked the roads into and out of Brea Ridge. We will find them."

"Thank you." I was impressed that they'd worked so quickly to get these measures into place.

Ben arrived. He shook Officer Hayden's hand before hugging me. Since I was still hugging Violet, his embrace encompassed us both.

The phone rang, and we all stiffened.

Officer McAfee held up a hand. "Everybody quiet! Ms. Armstrong, answer the call, and put it on speaker. We need to hear everything that's being said as well as any background noise."

Ben and I stepped back from Violet. Her little face was so wan and haunted.

I squeezed her shoulders as the phone rang again. "It'll be okay."

She nodded, answered the phone, and put it on speaker. Jason moved over to hold her hand.

The caller was using something to make his voice sound mechanical and unrecognizable. "Mrs. Armstrong, your children miss you."

"Please let me talk with them! I need to know they're all right!"

"Not quite yet. But, rest assured, they are fine. At the moment."

"We'll do anything you want," Violet said. "Please just don't hurt my babies."

McAfee slid a slip of paper across the table. It said, Ask him what he wants.

"Wh-what do you want?" Violet asked.

"I want your sister to call off her wedding."

Everyone looked at me as if I'd suddenly grown a second head.

"Done," I said, loudly enough so the caller could hear. McAfee looked aggravated that I'd spoken, but I didn't care. I went on. "The wedding is off. Now just bring the children home or tell us where we can pick them up."

"You talk a good game, but I want assurances," said the caller. "I want your marriage license. You have it already, don't you?"

"Yes, but it isn't with me," I said. "I'll get it and exchange it to you for Lucas and Leslie."

The line went dead.

"What was that?" Officer Hayden asked.

"Is there something you'd like to tell us, Ms. Martin?" McAfee put an uncomfortable distance between the two of us. "Your ex-husband shows up and then ends up murdered in his hotel room. His alleged partner is found shot to death. And now your niece and nephew have been kidnapped. And all of this somehow involves your wedding."

Ben put a protective arm around me. "Just a minute. This isn't Daphne's fault. She didn't ask for Todd to victimize her yet again. And she certainly wouldn't put Lucas and Leslie in danger for anything."

"I'm not saying this is her fault," said Officer McAfee. "I'm just wondering if there's a secret admirer we don't know about." He addressed me. "Have you had any phone calls, anonymous letters or gifts, anyone acting differently toward you?"

"No." I looked at Violet and Jason. "I swear, I don't have any idea why this person wants me to call off my wedding, but I'll do whatever it takes to get the kids back safe and sound."

"I know," she whispered.

"We have to go on the assumption that the caller hung up in order to give you time to get the marriage license and that he'll call back." Hayden joined the now tight circle that included me, Ben, and McAfee. "Do you already have the license or were you bluffing?"

"I have it," said Ben.

"Can you get to it quickly?" asked McAfee.

"Yeah."

"Good." McAfee walked back to the center of the room, giving us a little breathing space. "When the kidnapper calls back, we'll tell him we have the document, and we'll set up the swap."

"Hopefully, we'll be able to catch him then," Hayden said.

McAfee shot his partner a dirty look, making me guess that Hayden wasn't supposed to have said that. Still, I knew the man was just trying to reassure Violet and Jason.

A wave of weariness washed over me. Ben must've felt it because he moved me over to the sofa and had me sit down. He sat beside me, and I rested my head against his shoulder. If only I could go to sleep, wake up, and tell Leslie and Lucas about this horrible dream I'd had in which they'd been kidnapped.

* * *

Before we heard from the kidnapper again, Myra, Mark, and China all showed up at the Armstrong house. We learned that China had heard the Amber Alert go out over the police scanner and had gone to Myra's house. Mark was still there, so they all came to Violet's house together.

"You say you heard about the Amber Alert over the scanner?" Officer McAfee asked China.

"Yeah, but if you're worried about the roadblocks, that information didn't go out."

He frowned. "Then how do you know?"

"Because it only makes sense," she said. "If you didn't put roadblocks in place, you're an idiot. I know good and well that you aren't an idiot, Mac."

He chuckled. "I appreciate that. All right, Ms. York. We all know you can think like the police. Think like the kidnapper. What does he want?"

"Well, I've been pondering that. What has he said he wants?"

McAfee nodded in our direction. "Their marriage license. He doesn't want Ben and Daphne getting married."

China looked up at the ceiling. "All right. Let's set out everything we know for certain. First, Daphne was targeted by a scam artist. Then her ex-husband showed up. After Todd got killed, we found out he and Monty were working together to sabotage the wedding. Now, even after they're both dead, there's still somebody out there who wants nothing more than to stop this wedding."

Violet gasped. "The man who murdered Todd and his partner has my babies?!" She screamed.

"We don't know that." Jason took Violet firmly by the shoulders. "You have to stop thinking the worst!"

It tore another piece of my heart to shreds to see Jason break down in tears and Violet cling to him.

"Todd's gone," I said. "And there's no more money to be had from wedding planning or any of that. What possible reason would anyone have to not want Ben and me to get married?"

"Maybe it's that old girlfriend of yours," Myra said to Ben. "This might not be about Daphne at all."

A few months ago, Ben's former college flame—Nickie Zane—had launched a new magazine called All Up in Your Business. She was a widow now and had made him a lucrative deal to come work for her in Kentucky. He'd ultimately turned her down and proposed to me.

He was clearly irritated that Myra had brought the subject up now. "I highly doubt Nickie would have orchestrated

Todd's visit and Monty Harlow's deception in order to stop my wedding to Daphne."

"I agree," said Mark. "The question we must answer is who would benefit if your marriage didn't take place."

China tapped her fingertips together. "The only way any scenario would make sense would be if it took one member of the equation completely out of the picture. What good would it do an admirer to stop the proceeding if the couple will just carry on as they were until another license is obtained? Whoever is behind this—"

She stopped, and I was certain she had been about to say that the person was desperate. But she didn't want to use that word when Violet and Jason were already so distraught.

Still, she was right. Whoever was doing this was desperate.

"You think he wants either Ben or me to leave Brea Ridge, don't you?" I asked China.

"That's exactly what I think."

"But why?"

Mark took Myra's hand, and together they walked toward the kitchen. He jerked his head slightly to indicate that Ben, China, and I should join them.

"What is it?" I asked.

"We need to work quickly. I know the police are doing all they can do, but it would be great if we could get some sort of idea of who's doing this."

"Agreed," said Ben.

"Daphne, who would benefit if you left Brea Ridge?" Mark asked me.

"I don't know. Another cake decorator, I suppose."

"Ben, same question."

Ben scoffed. "Neil Grant, I guess. He'd take over the top spot at the Chronicle."

"He was on the list," I murmured.

"What list?" Myra asked.

"The list of alumni from the University of Tennessee. I looked it up to see if there was anyone living here that Todd might've known from school."

"I'll start looking into this Neil Grant," said Mark. "Come on, Myra. Let's leave out the back."

"I'm coming with you," said China. "There's nothing more I can do here." She stopped in front of me and squeezed both my hands. "We will find them. We will."

CHAPTER NINETEEN

"I t just occurred to me that I didn't see Neil after lunch," Ben told me, as he took out his cell phone.

When his call went to voicemail, he called the receptionist at the Brea Ridge Chronicle and learned that Neil called in after lunch. He'd said he wasn't feeling well and was going home to rest.

"We need to talk with him." I glanced over my shoulder at Violet and Jason, who were talking with Officer Hayden. "I don't want to interrupt. Let's go out through the kitchen. I'll leave Violet a message saying that we're going out to look for the kids and to call us if they hear anything."

At Neil's apartment, our apprehension grew when he didn't answer the door. Fortunately, the supervisor was working at the apartment next door.

"Hey! Excuse me!" Ben called.

The stocky man, who had an air of irritability, blew out a breath as he turned. "What?"

"My friend Neil left work sick today, and now he isn't answering the door. Could you let us inside?"

"Maybe he went to the doctor."

While it was true that we didn't see Neil's car in the parking lot, we wanted to get into his apartment to see if there was any indication that he'd taken Lucas and Leslie.

"You can stay with us the whole time," I said. "We just want to make sure he isn't lying in there unconscious and in need of medical attention."

With a scowl, the manager lumbered over , flipped through some keys, and unlocked the door. "I don't have time to babysit you. If he ain't in there, you'd better be out in two minutes, or I'm calling the cops." He held up two stubby, dirty fingers. "Two minutes."

"Neil!" Ben called, for the benefit of the manager. "You here, buddy?"

The door opened into the living room. The apartment had an open floor plan. To the right of the living room was the kitchen. There was a hallway beyond the living room that led to bedrooms on either side. Ben took the room to the left, and I took the room to the right.

The room I entered was an office. One wall was almost entirely covered with corkboard. Pinned to it was a homemade poster with the heading "Master Plan." Beneath Neil's master plan was a list of his accomplishments: Complete high school with a 4.0 GPA. Attend UT. Graduate UT with a 4.0 GPA. Work on small newspaper. Become editor of small newspaper. Become editor of a larger newspaper. There were more items on the list, but those were enough to make me even more concerned than I was already.

There were checkmarks after the first two. "Graduate UT with a 4.0 GPA" had an asterisk after it and the note "3.85."

Surrounding the master plan were photos and mementos of his accomplishments. One clipping stood out. It was an announcement for All Up in Your Business magazine. Beside the announcement was an index card on which Neil had written, "Once Ben leaves Brea Ridge for this gig, the editor position is mine. Biding my time."

"Ben, let's go!" I hurried into the hallway. "We have to find Neil. I think he has Lucas and Leslie."

"Why? What'd you find?"

I told him what I'd seen, and we hurried back outside. I ran headlong into the manager who'd used his "two minutes" to grab a cold beer. The bottle was open, and when we collided, he spilled the entire thing all over me.

"Geez, lady, watch where you're going."

I glared at him momentarily and headed for Ben's Jeep.

"You call Mark while I drive," he said. "We'll run by your house so you can change your shirt."

Mark was listed in my contacts, so I was able to reach him quickly. "Ben and I went to Neil's apartment. He wasn't there, but we had the supervisor let us in. I found evidence that he wants to be editor of the Chronicle. I think he's hoping to derail the wedding in the hope that Ben will reconsider taking the job with Nickie Zane."

"I discovered that Neil has a half-brother who graduated with Todd. His name is Harry Richmond, and I was just getting ready to go see him."

"Where?"

"He works as a waiter at Dakota's."

"Head to Dakota's," I told Ben. "We'll meet you there, Mark."

Ben pulled into my driveway, and I barely waited for him to put the vehicle in park before I hopped out and hurried to the door. I went inside and began removing the sopping, smelly blouse. A button popped off and rolled under the island.

"Darn! I need to find that so Sparrow or Sally doesn't swallow it," I said.

I had to get on all fours and crawl up under the island to reach the button. I grabbed the button and happened to look up. Secured to the underside of the island was a tiny black box.

Using my nails to pry off the box. Examining it, I scooted out from under the island, stood, and took the device over to the counter where I could get a better look at it. I wasn't sure what it was, but the thought that it could be some sort of listening transmitter gave me goosebumps.

I hurried into the bathroom and washed the sticky beer off my torso.

The thought occurred to me—could they see me as well? I shuddered and tried to hustle.

Leaving the blouse in the bathtub, I hurried to the bedroom, shed my bra, and tossed it into the hamper. As quickly as I could, I put on a clean bra and t-shirt.

When I returned to the kitchen, Ben was staring at the tiny black box. He put his finger to his lips. "Let's go." He ushered me out the door. "If I'm not mistaken, that's a listening device."

"That's what I thought too."

"But, first things first. Let's worry about Lucas and Leslie, and we'll deal with whatever that little black box is as soon as the kids are safe."

* * *

When Ben and I arrived at Dakota's, Mark, Myra, and China were already there. The hostess put us at a table that seated six. As she walked away, Mark said, "I've already requested Harry as our server."

"Thanks," Ben said.

I wondered briefly what Harry had taken in college that had led him to a job here at Dakota's. Maybe he was forced to work a second job because the one for which he'd earned his degree didn't pay enough.

Moments later, Harry joined us. He was tall and thin with shoulder-length, dark blond hair, and he looked nothing like Neil. I'd have never made a connection between the two of them without knowing they were half-brothers.

"Hey, there. I'm Harry, and I'll be your server today. What can I start you off with to drink?"

"Actually, we'd like to talk with you about your brother Neil," said Mark.

Harry stiffened. "Half-brother."

I stood to better appeal to him. "Please. We think Neil might have kidnapped my niece and nephew. Do you think he's capable of doing something like that?"

"It's possible. Neil has some emotional problems. But, rest assured, if he has the kids, he won't hurt them."

That would be easier to believe if we weren't pretty sure that Neil had killed Todd and Monty.

"Why do you say that?" asked China.

"Because I know Neil," said Harry. "Yeah, he gets crazy sometimes and does things that make no sense to anyone except him, but he's never been violent toward anyone or anything. He isn't dangerous."

"If he did take the kids, where would he go?" Myra asked. "Ben and Daphne have checked, and they aren't at Neil's apartment."

"He'd take them somewhere they'd feel safe. Have you tried calling him?"

"Yes," said Ben. "But he isn't answering."

"Let me try." Harry put down his pad and pen and got out his cell phone. He punched in Neil's number. After a pause, he said, "Hey, Neil. Where are you, buddy?" Pause. "Anybody with you?" Pause. "That's good, man, but their parents are worried. I'll have them come meet you there, okay?" He ended the call. "They're at the movie theater in Bristol."

"Thank God." I took out my phone. "I'll let Violet know."

* * *

Leslie and Lucas were smiling when they emerged from the theater. When they spotted all of us waiting, they both ran to embrace Ben.

"Thanks so much for treating us to pizza and a movie, Uncle Ben!" said Lucas. "I was feeling left out since I can't go to the bachelor party, and this more than made up for it."

"And thank you for including me too," Leslie said. "Uncle Neil said you wanted to do something special for the two of us." She looked around. "Where is he, by the way?"

"He had to go talk with some people," said Jason.

Violet enveloped both of her children in a hug once they'd let go of Ben. She held them and cried.

"Gosh, Mom." Lucas scoffed. "We weren't gone that long."

"It felt like forever," she said.

Ben's contact at the precinct later told us that Neil vowed that he had nothing to do with the deaths of Todd Martin and Monty Harlow. He claimed to know nothing about the plot to swindle me. But, then again, he'd also tried to pass off taking the twins for pizza and a movie as a "nice gesture."

He said he knew Ben was busy and that Ben would've suggested it had he thought of it. He hadn't realized Violet would be so concerned.

When confronted with the fact that he'd called Violet and made demands, he said he'd only been joking. The Brea Ridge Police Department did not find his antics amusing. He'd been charged with kidnapping and extortion and was in jail awaiting arraignment.

In my mind, I pictured Neil. Short, a tad on the pudgy side, brown hair, blue eyes, glasses...usually wearing khakis, a polo, and loafers. He appeared to be the personification of mild mannered. And yet, he'd kidnapped my sister's children.

Granted, they never knew they'd been kidnapped. But who knows what would've happened after the movie? Would Neil have bound and gagged Lucas and Leslie had they started wanting to go home? Harry had told us that Neil wasn't violent but that he was emotionally unbalanced.

If Neil was telling the truth and hadn't murdered Todd and Monty, then their killer was still out there. And I had no idea whether or not he still wanted something.

* * *

With the crisis averted, Ben went back to work to finish up a few things and to decide what to tell his staff about Neil.

Obviously, the assistant editor wouldn't be back in the office, so the staff had to be told something. But Ben wasn't exactly sure what to say. He told me he'd think about it on the way.

He also had to decide whether or not to run the story of the kidnapping in the Chronicle. He didn't want Lucas or Leslie to realize that they'd been in danger. And we didn't have the full story yet about Neil's mental state and whether or not he was capable of violence. But, even though the Amber Alert had been rescinded, the residents of Brea Ridge needed to know why every road leading out of the town had been blocked yesterday.

Leaving Ben to wrestle with his problems, I went home to work on the wedding cake. I had two days to assemble and decorate the cake. Mark and Myra came with me so he could look at the black box to determine whether or not Ben had been right about it being a bug.

Once we were in the kitchen, I whistled and banged pans around as if I was working. If there was someone listening to me, we didn't want him to know I was wise to him.

If I'd thought my acting nonchalant was bad, I quickly realized that I wasn't in it with Myra.

"Hello, Daphne, our dear friend!" She winked as if I needed to be clued in as to what she was doing. "How relieved we are that the children were found alive and well at the cinema! Mark and I thought we should come over and see if you and Ben would like to go out and enjoy a celebratory dinner with us."

I pointed out the device to Mark. He examined it and nodded.

Myra's eyes got as big as saucers. "So! Daphne! What do you say? To dinner, I mean."

"I'd love to?" I looked at Mark.

He nodded.

"Yes! I'd love to!" If anyone was listening, he surely thought that Myra and I were idiots.

We stepped outside to the carport.

"What do you think?" I whispered to Mark.

"It's definitely a listening device." He spoke in a normal voice. "I want you to leave it as is for now. I'm going to contact Ben and see if his friend on the police force can let me look at the cell phones of Neil, Todd, and Monty. I can tell whether any of those cell phones have the software for the device installed on their phones."

"That's how this person has been listening to me? Through a cell phone?"

"Most likely." He turned and kissed Myra. "I'll grab a burger on the way. You two go and have a good dinner."

"I don't think so! I'll call China and see if she can bring that shotgun of hers over here. If there's anybody listening on that thing in there, we just told them that Daphne wasn't going to be home."

"That's right. I'll stay here in the carport." I unfolded a plastic rocking chair and sat down to hammer home my point. "You two go on to dinner and then to the jail or wherever. I'll wait here."

Myra wasn't having that. "Mark, you run me to town, and we'll get us all some burgers. Then you bring me back here and drop me off. You can call me on my cell as soon as you and Ben know something."

CHAPTER TWENTY

aving China bring the shotgun and our keeping vigil on the carport had done us no good whatsoever yesterday. When Mark and Ben got to my house, they said that no cell phone had been found on Todd, and neither of the ones on Monty or Neil had the transmitter software installed.

The general consensus was that Todd had stuck the bug under the counter when he'd come to my house that day. The software must have been on his phone, which had not been in his hotel room when he was taken to the morgue. That meant that now either someone else had his phone or the phone was in Todd's truck in the impound yard.

Either way, I had a wedding cake to finish and no time to worry about things that could possibly go wrong. At least no one was eavesdropping on us now. Mark had taken a hammer and smashed the listening device to bits.

It was now half past four in the afternoon, and I'd been working on the cake all day. I had the tiers iced, covered in fondant, and stacked. In addition, I'd done the Australian string work on three out of five of the tiers.

I stretched and admired my work. The cake was looking great, if I did say so myself. Although, I didn't actually say it—I just thought it.

Ben and the guys were enjoying the bachelor party tonight. That meant that after I got the cake finished, I could soak in the bathtub for at least thirty minutes, get out, and put on my fluffy white robe—so what if it was August? I had the air conditioner on. Plus, I could eat ice cream right from the carton. And I could watch some sappy love story or a crime drama—no, scratch that. I'd had enough crime and drama this week. I'd go with a romantic comedy.

I massaged my tiring hands for a minute, and then I picked up my piping bag. As I twirled the cake on the turntable and piped the bottom border on the second to the top tier, the song lyrics, "round and around we go" popped into my head. I couldn't for the life of me remember the name of the song or any of the rest of the lyrics. Maybe I'd been smelling sugar for too long.

Anyway, I'd just finished piping that border when someone knocked on the side door. I figured it was Myra.

"Come on in!" I called.

The doorknob rattled. "Can't." It was a male voice—an unfamiliar male voice. "It's locked."

"Just a minute then." I put down the piping bag and went to the door. It was Jeff, McElroy Haynes' worker. I didn't open the door. "Is Mr. Haynes making you bug me again?"

"Not this time," he said with a grin. "I was just in the area working on another stove, and I thought I ought to stop by and make sure everything is all right with yours. I know tomorrow is your wedding, and I don't want you to be inconvenienced on the big day."

"No chance. The cake is almost finished."

"Can I see it?"

I felt silly saying no, but there was something about this guy that was suddenly making the hair on the back of my neck stand up. "Sure. Come to the wedding tomorrow."

"Aw, you won't let me get a peek at it before then?"

"Afraid not," I said. "No one gets to see the cake before the big day—except me, of course."

The grin disappeared. "Let me in, Daphne."

"No, and if you don't get off my porch right now, I'm calling the police."

"By the time they get here, you'll be dead." He raised his hand to show me that he held a gun.

I ducked and moved farther into the kitchen. Before I could reach my phone, Jeff shot the window of the door. Glass flew back into the room. Irrationally, I was glad that the cake wasn't in the direct line of fire.

Or maybe it wasn't such an irrational thought. I'd worked hard on that cake.

Why hadn't I put on my telephone headset today? Because I hadn't wanted to be disturbed, that's why. That hadn't turned out well.

I looked around the kitchen for my cell phone and realized I must've left it in the living room. Running to the living room, I heard the doorknob jiggling in the kitchen. Jeff must've been able to knock out enough of the window to get his hand through and unlock the door.

He was quick. Before I could get to my phone, he tackled me.

I fought, but I was no match for him. He pinned my arms to my sides and lay on top of me. I thrashed until my limbs were rubbery.

"Please. You have to go. My fiancé will be here any minute."

"You're lying. I know the bachelor party is this evening."

"The bug. It was you."

"Actually, it was your stupid ex-husband," Jeff said. "Why he didn't smack you around that day he came here and make him give you the ring is beyond me."

"That's what all this is about? His grandmother's engagement ring?" I scoffed. "That thing probably came from a five-and-dime store. If it had been worth anything, do you think Todd would've given it to me?"

"It was worth something—is worth something—over ten thousand dollars to be exact."

"You're insane." I had a flash of inspiration. "But if you'll let me up, I'll get you the stupid ring."

"Get it. And be quick about it." Jeff rolled off of me and jerked me to my feet. He took the gun out of the back of his jeans where he'd apparently stashed it before he tackled me.

"There's no need for that. I'll give you the ring. And then, please, just leave." I headed toward the bedroom. "How did you know Todd anyway?"

He followed me down the hall. "He and Monty were in the pen with my brother. When they got into that mess selling stolen electronics, they called to see if I could help them come up with something else." He snorted. "Todd promised he could set me up in some kind of construction scam, but that was a lie. He couldn't do jack."

"Is that why you killed him?" I looked back over my shoulder at Jeff as I stepped across the threshold into the bedroom.

"He and Monty were both worthless. I simply put both those jerks out of their misery." He waved the gun toward the empty room. "Get me that ring."

Opening my jewelry box, I prayed I had a ring I could pass off as Todd's heirloom.

"Nobody move! This is the police!"

The shout came from the kitchen. Stunned, Jeff whirled toward the sound. I took that opportunity to grab a bookend off the chest of drawers and bash him on the back of the head.

"Ow!"

As he turned back toward me, I hit him again—this time in the face. He crumpled to the floor, dropping the gun and holding his nose.

I scooped up the gun and raced toward the kitchen. "Thank God you're here! How'd you know? Did Myra call you?" I shook my head. "It doesn't matter. He's in there."

"He? Darlin', I'm here for you!" The officer whipped out an mp3 player, clicked a button, and burlesque music began to play. He stripped off his shirt as he danced around.

I made a lunge for the handcuffs I spotted at the side of his pants.

"Don't be so impatient! I'll be here for an hour." He smiled and continued dancing.

"I need those cuffs!"

"All right. But it'll cost extra." He handed me the handcuffs.

Before I could run into the bedroom and cuff Jeff—which in hindsight wouldn't have worked very well because they were probably kid's handcuffs—Myra, China, and Juanita burst into the kitchen yelling, "Surprise!"

They were the ones surprised, though, because at that moment, Jeff came running out of the bedroom yelling obscenities.

Strippy Cop was surprised too. "Aw, heck no! I didn't sign up for this. I'm out!"

"Then you ain't getting paid!" Myra yelled at the half-naked man who pushed past her and out the kitchen door.

"You shut up and freeze!" China yelled at Jeff. She'd pulled out a pistol from somewhere. "Y'all get behind me!" She cocked the gun. "Except you. You move one more quarter of an inch, and I'll blow you plumb back into that bedroom."

I later learned that China had this gun in an ankle holster just in case because, you know, the killer hadn't been caught yet. Thank goodness for China and her penchant for firearms.

With Jeff immobilized, I was finally able to get to my phone and call the police. The real police.

* * *

So Myra had been planning a surprise bachelorette party. It had certainly been a surprise—for all concerned. Poor Strippy Cop. I told Myra I'd pay his bill because had it not been for him, Jeff might've killed me.

"I'll pay him," she said with a sigh. "Even though I didn't get to see his butt in some of them silky drawers they wear."

"How do you know what they wear?" China asked.

"I've seen 'em on television." She scowled. "I really did want to see his butt."

"What if it had been a disappointment?" I tried to hide my smile. "Now he'll always have the perfect butt because you'll never know if it wasn't."

Juanita was blushing. "Your cake is beautiful, Daphne."

"Oh, my goodness." I hopped up off the sofa and ran to check on it. Despite everything, it still looked great. I nearly collapsed in relief.

China chuckled. "Somebody up there likes you."

All three women had followed me.

I slowly turned the cake. "Are we sure there's no glass in it?"

"There couldn't be," Myra said. "We swept up all the glass, and there wasn't any anywhere near the island."

"You're positive?" I asked.

"Yes."

"Thank you all for cleaning up while I talked with the police." I hugged each of them. "I'm sorry your party turned into such a disaster."

"It's your party," said China. "And it's not a total disaster, is it?"

I smiled. "I guess not."

"Of course, it's not." Juanita got out her phone. "I'll order pizza, and while we wait for the food to get here, we can watch you finish decorating the cake."

"But— "

"Good idea," interrupted Myra. "And then we can eat and watch a movie. Maybe we can find one where some good-looking man wears silky drawers."

I laughed and cried all at once. "You guys are impossible. Thank you."

Know the best part? We managed to keep everything from the guys until both parties were over.

* * *

The Fremont home was modeled after Crane Cottage on Jekyll Island. Like the largest private residence on the island situated off the Georgia coast, this house was built in the Italian Renaissance style. Mom was right—Belinda Fremont did love to entertain and to show off that house. Who could blame her?

Ben and I were getting married in the replica formal garden. Hedges trimmed in a repeating diamond pattern framed the left and right sides of the garden leading to a crescent-shaped fountain surrounded by a bed of flowers.

In the upper right corner of the garden, a string quartet played "Canon in D" as Leslie and Violet walked down the aisle between the rows of white folding chairs. They switched to "The Wedding March" as my dad and I started down the aisle. Everyone stood, of course, but I could see a small enclosure in the front left where it wouldn't be obscured by the wedding party.

I smiled. Although I couldn't really make them out from this far away, I knew that six Satin Peruvian guinea pigs—or cavies—were inside the wire bordered enclosure trimmed with white ribbon so that they could enjoy the wedding.

I glanced over at Dad.

"What's that?" he asked. "Are they releasing doves or something afterward?"

I stifled a laugh. "No. I'll explain later."

Then I caught sight of Ben. He was looking at me with such love in his eyes. He was my destiny.

I squeezed Dad's arm. Having him beside me was the only reason I hadn't kicked off my shoes and sprinted the rest of the way to Ben's side.

Well, Dad and the fact that it might astonish the cavies.

* * *

The reception was winding down when Mom finally came to hug me and talk with me alone.

"I'm sorry for all that business about Todd," she said quietly. "I didn't mean to invite him back into your life."

"It's okay, Mom. That's all in the past. Besides, he didn't want back into my life. He wanted my money and his grandmother's ring." I shook my head. "I don't know how he got it into his head—or into the head of the man who killed him over it—that it was worth so much."

"It was worth a lot. Before you and Todd were—" She lowered her voice to a whisper. "—married—" She resumed speaking normally as if she'd said a bad word she couldn't say at my current reception. "His mother explained that the ring was an Art Deco ring made in the 1920s."

"Really? Huh. And to think I shipped it back to his mother in a bubble-wrap lined envelope and didn't even insure it." I smiled. "Todd was so stingy I wouldn't have thought he'd ever give me something so valuable."

"I believe he loved you once." She held up a hand. "I know that's not something you want to hear."

"No, actually, it's a comfort. It makes me feel that the years I spent with him weren't completely wasted." I hugged her. "I love you, Mom."

"I love you, my sweet girl."

And then the man of my dreams stole me away for another dance.

- END -

AUTHOR'S NOTE

Dear Reader:

I hope you enjoyed Killer Wedding Cake. I have fun writing about the Brea Ridge characters and all of their adventures.

When the series was released by its previous publisher after *Battered to Death*, many of you wrote to ask about the next book. I'm happy to be able to present it to you at long last. Please let me know what you thought about *Killer Wedding Cake*—what you liked, what you didn't like, what you'd like to see more of, and what you'd like to see less of. I'd love your feedback. My email address is gayle@gayletrent.com.

Also, as you probably know, reviews are hard to come by. You, the reader, have the power to make or break a book. If you have the time, would you please visit my author page on Amazon (http://bit.ly/KillerWeddingCake) and leave a review of *Killer Wedding Cake*? Whether you loved the book or hated it, I'd still like to get your opinion.

Thanks for reading *Killer Wedding Cake* and for spending time with me and the Brea Ridge gang.

More importantly, if you or someone you know might be living in an abusive situation, please visit the following links:

http://www.helpguide.org/articles/abuse/domestic-violence-and-abuse.htm

http://www.thehotline.org/

http://www.ncadv.org/

Best wishes,

Gayle

ABOUT THE AUTHOR

Gayle Trent (and pseudonym Amanda Lee) writes the Daphne Martin Cake Decorating series and the Embroidery Mystery series.

The cake decorating series features a heroine who is starting her life over in Southwest Virginia after a nasty divorce. The heroine, Daphne, has returned to her hometown of Brea Ridge to open a cake baking and decorating business and is wrestling with the question of whether or not one can go home again.

Gayle lives in Virginia with her family, including the Great Pyrenees "lap dog" pictured with her above.

DAPHNE'S KITCHEN

CITRON VODKA CAKE

(Submitted by Kerry Vincent—Above Illustration
by Kerry Vincent)

Ingredients:
250-g (1/2 lb.) 2 sticks butter softened
440g (14 oz) 2 cups of sugar
4 large eggs
620g (20 oz) 3 1/4 C plain (all purpose) flour
1 t salt
1 t baking powder
1/2 t soda
1 t vanilla essence (extract)
2 t lemon essence (extract)

Juice of one large lemon (60ml) (2oz) (1/4 C) zest of two
250ml (8 oz)(1 cup) of buttermilk

Preparation:

Grease1 x 25cm x 8cm (1 x 10 x3 inch) or Bundt pan
Set oven 170C (325F) (GM3)
Cream butter and sugar till light and fluffy. Add vanilla.
Add eggs one at a time beating after each addition
Sift dry ingredients and add alternately with buttermilk,
start and end with flour. Mix 2 minutes medium speed. Add
lemon juice and zest.

Cook on the middle rack of the oven for 60 - 65- minutes -
- for three-inch deep pans... check earlier around 45 minutes if
the mixture is divided between 2 x10-inch pans.

Test with a skewer before removing from the oven.
Immediately prick the cake all over with a satay stick and
pour over lemon vodka sauce. This will not hurt the cake as
the holes will fill with the sauce and the cake crumb will
absorb the liquid and begin to swell. About ten minutes before
the cake is ready to come out of the oven mix the following
ingredients.

LEMON VODKA SAUCE

260g (8oz) 1 Cup sugar
125g 1/4 lb. butter
2 teaspoons lemon essence (extract)
Juice of one lemon then make up to half a cup with
Stolichnaya Lemon (Citron) Vodka. Do not substitute.

Heat together, just enough to melt the butter. Do not boil.
Pour over the hot cake and do not remove from pan until it is

almost cold. This cake is extremely rich, very delicious and not for anyone watching their calories.

Serve slices with a light dusting of powdered sugar, and on the side a teaspoonful of raspberry jam and a dollop of whipped cream.

TIPS: If the cake sticks when turning it out that simply means it was left too long in the pan and the sauce has set. All is not lost put the cake back in a warm oven for a few minutes to melt the sauce or heat the exterior surface with a hair dryer set on hot.

Use one set of measurements, metric, imperial or dip and sweep – do not mix and match!

Died and gone to heaven!!!

CHOCOLATE PISTACHIO CAKE

Ingredients:

1 pkg. white or yellow cake mix

1 pkg. pistachio pudding mix

½ cup orange juice

½ cup water

4 eggs

½ cup oil

¾ cup chocolate syrup

Preparation:

Preheat oven to 350 degrees.

Combine cake mix, pistachio pudding mix, orange juice, water, eggs and oil in large mixing bowl. Blend to moisten, and then beat for two minutes at medium speed with electric mixer.

Pour approximately ¾ batter into well-greased and floured Bundt or tube pan. Add chocolate syrup to remaining batter. Mix well. Pour over batter in pan.

Bake at 350 degrees F for about one hour.

SPICY PUMPKIN ROLL
(Makes 2 Rolls)

Ingredients:

6 eggs, separated

1 cup all-purpose flour

1 cup canned pumpkin

2 tsp. ground cinnamon

1 tsp. baking powder

1 tsp. ginger

½ tsp. nutmeg

½ tsp. salt

1 cup sugar

Confectioner's sugar

Preparation:

Mix egg yolks, flour, pumpkin, cinnamon, baking powder, ginger, nutmeg, salt, and remaining sugar. In large bowl with mixer on high speed, beat egg whites until soft peaks form. Beating at high speed, gradually beat in ½ cup sugar until sugar is dissolved. Whites should stand in stiff, glossy peaks. With wire whisk or spatula, gently fold pumpkin mixture into egg white mixture.

Grease 15 ½" x 10" jelly roll pan, line with waxed paper, grease and flour paper.

Spread half of batter evenly in jelly roll pan, set remaining batter aside. Bake for 12 minutes or until top of cake springs back when touched with finger.

When cake is done, immediately invert onto towel that has been dusted with confectioner's sugar. Starting at narrow end, roll cake with towel, jelly roll fashion. Place cake, seam-side down, on wire rack. Cool for about 1 ½ hours.

While cake is cooling, reline jelly roll pan and bake remaining batter.

Filling

Ingredients
2 8-oz. packages cream cheese
3 cups confectioner's sugar
½ tsp. salt
Chopped walnuts (optional)

Preparation
In small bowl, mix all ingredients at low speed until blended.

After preparing filling, gently unroll cooled cakes. Evenly spread half of cream cheese mixture on each cake almost to edges. Starting at the same narrow end, reroll each cake without the towel. Place rolls seam-side down on large platter. Cover and refrigerate until chilled (about 1 hour).

To Freeze

Wrap each pumpkin roll tightly with foil or freezer wrap, seal, and freeze for up to one month. To thaw, let rolls stay wrapped in refrigerator for about 3 hours.

To serve, sprinkle rolls lightly with confectioner's sugar.

CPSIA information can be obtained at www.ICGtesting.com
Printed in the USA
LVOW06s1841130815

450005LV00019B/737/P